NOAH'S CASTLE

BOOKS BY JOHN ROWE TOWNSEND

Forest of the Night

Written for Children

Modern Poetry

The Summer People

A Sense of Story

Good Night, Prof, Dear

The Intruder

Trouble in the Jungle
(originally *Gumble's Yard*)

Pirate's Island

Good-bye to the Jungle

NOAH'S CASTLE

JOHN ROWE TOWNSEND

J. B. LIPPINCOTT COMPANY
Philadelphia and New York

U. S. Library of Congress Cataloging in Publication Data

Townsend, John Rowe.
  Noah's castle.

  SUMMARY: A family struggles to survive in a desperate time when the
framework of life as they know it is rapidly being destroyed.
  [1. Conduct of life—Fiction. 2. Fathers and sons—Fiction] I. Title.
PZ7.T6637No3   [Fic]   75-30709
ISBN-0-397-31654-2

FOR PENNY, WHO RETAINS HER VALUE

AUTHOR'S NOTE

This story is set in a future which you can
suppose to be two or three years after the
time at which you are reading it. But I am
not predicting that the conditions it de-
scribes will actually come about. It is a
work of fiction, not of forecasting.

J. R. T.

NOAH'S CASTLE

1

IT WAS JUST LIKE MY FATHER. He hadn't told anyone what he was up to. He came downstairs that Sunday morning as usual at nine o'clock sharp, glanced at the clock, cast an eye around the breakfast table to see that everyone was present and dressed, took a bowl of cereal from my mother's hands, and said, "Well. This morning I've something to show you all. Be ready in half an hour."

My younger sister, Ellen, aged ten, asked, "Are we going in the car?"

"Yes," said Father.

"Can we take Peggy?" (Peggy was Ellen's dog.)

"No," said Father.

My brother Geoff, aged fifteen, asked, "How long shall we be away?"

"As long as it takes," said Father.

My elder sister, Nessie, aged seventeen, said, "If it's going to take long I'm not coming. I promised I'd go round to a friend's house this morning."

"Agnes," my father said, "I am . . ." A pause. ". . . Requesting you to come with us. Everyone is coming. There's something I want you to see."

"But what shall I say to Pauline?"

"You can telephone her. You can say what you like. It's not for me to tell you what to say to your friends. I should have thought the truth would serve as well as anything. But I'll be . . ." Another pause. ". . . Obliged if you'll be ready at half past nine like the rest of us."

"Nobody else my age . . ." Nessie began.

"Agnes," my father said, very quietly, "I have asked you if you will kindly come with us, and I hope you will."

Nessie opened her mouth to say something, but thought better of it, and the conversation was at an end.

Later I found I was drying the dishes for Mother. We had a roster for household duties, drawn up by Father, and Sunday was the day it was changed.

"What's he going to show us?" I asked her.

"It's no good asking me," Mother said. "You should know by now, he doesn't tell me anything."

"Well, he ought to, oughtn't he?"

"You know what he is," Mother said.

"He thinks he's still in the army."

"Not now, he doesn't."

It was more than thirty years since Father had been in the army. He'd served all through the Hitler war, and been made an officer just as it ended; not bad for a man who'd left school at fourteen without any certificates. It was the height of Father's career. We knew he sometimes wished he could have stayed on in the regular army. Managing a shop was a comedown. Managing the same shop, year after year, was a disappointment he'd never been reconciled to.

"He can't go on treating us this way, you know," I said. "Nessie won't stand for it much longer."

"Don't talk like that," my mother said. "Not about your father."

"As soon as she's earning, she'll go."

"Hurry up with those dishes, Barry, or we'll be late."

"Late for what?"

"You heard what he said. Half past nine."

Nessie had come in while we were talking.

"Mother, I despair of you," she said. But Mother was taking her apron off, not listening.

It was September. Back-to-school time, back-to-work time. The holidays, endless-seeming in July and August, had shrunk to snapshot-size memories. The world was closing in again. The headlines were full of economic gloom, ever-rising prices, political squabbles. "Winter is icumen in," our English teacher had told us wittily. The weather wasn't too sure about that, for we were having a run of clear blue days. But the leaves were innumerable shades of yellow, green, and brown, and the air cooled quickly in the evenings.

We were late starting after all, that Sunday. Father sat on at the breakfast table while we waited, ready to go. He was studying the Sunday newspaper. More gloom. Bread up, meat up, milk going up any day now. They had all doubled in price since last year. But Father's expression was strange. There was a kind of grim satisfaction in it.

"Right," he said at last. "We'll be on our way." But he still didn't tell us where we were going.

Father got the car out. Mother didn't drive, and Father wouldn't let Nessie learn, although she was old enough. He didn't think much of women drivers. The car was five years old, but it was in lovely condition. Father maintained it himself. "You can't trust garages to do the job properly," he used to say. "Employing too many young lads these days. They don't care."

The journey took twenty minutes. Father, driving meticulously as always, took us through the city center, traffic-free in the Sunday morning peace, out to the other side of town, and up the Mount. The Mount is a high, leafy suburb where rich merchants and manufacturers lived in Victorian times. Nowadays they've mostly sold out, and those who are still in business live many miles away, in deep country. But the old houses were built to last, and last they do. Most have been converted into apartments.

Near the top of the Mount we turned into a gravel drive between stone gateposts, from which hung a pair of peeling wooden gates, propped open and leaning at an angle. One of them bore, in Gothic lettering, the name ROSE GROVE. The drive, neglected and weedy, disappeared into a thicket of dark, drooping evergreens and took two or three twists and turns in a very short distance. Then we were at the house. It wasn't really far from the road; you could hear the traffic clearly; but it was as if somebody had tried to make it as remote as a limited amount of space allowed.

It was a squarish house, not big but brutal. A solid house of hard red brick, ugly as sin. The windows were narrow, not much more than slits. There was a massive front porchway, with double doors that seemed intended to keep people out rather than to open and welcome them in. A crest of battlements. An enormous sign, FOR SALE.

"Well, here we are," Father said. He got out of the car. We followed and stood in a little group, just behind him.

"For sale," my mother read out—unnecessarily, since the letters were about a foot high. A pause. Then, "Who'd want that?"

"I suppose it could be turned into flats," I said.

"It's like a fort," said Nessie.

"A castle," said Geoff. "Look at those battlements. You could shoot with bows and arrows from behind there. Or mount guns, even. Or pour boiling oil on people."

"Don't be horrid," Ellen said, shuddering.

My mother's train of thought was different. "I can't think who'd buy *this*," she said.

There was a glint in my father's eye, a glint of pride and satisfaction.

"It's not for sale anymore," he said.

"You mean it's sold?"

"Yes, it's sold."

"Somebody with more money than sense, I should think," my mother said. A frown crossed Father's face, but a moment later the satisfied gleam returned. And suddenly I knew.

I looked across at Nessie, who opened her eyes wide in an expression of comic dismay. She knew, too.

"You haven't . . .?" I asked Father.

"Yes, I have."

"You've bought it?"

"Yes, indeed!" Father said proudly. "It's my house now. We move in next month."

My mother gasped.

"Norman!" she said. Her dismay was not comic. She paused, and then went on with a flat recklessness. "You *can't* have. You must be out of your mind."

My father's eyes narrowed. "That's enough, May," he said in the quiet voice that usually shut any of us up.

But Mother was roused now.

"It's far too big for us," she said. "How could we furnish and carpet a place like this? Think what the taxes would be. Think of keeping up the garden. You must be joking."

"I never joke," Father said in the quiet voice. "Pull yourself together, May. I've bought it, and you might as well start getting used to the idea. *I'll* deal with the problems."

"Bought it without consulting me," Mother said.

"Consult *you?*" Father seemed amused by the idea. "I didn't need to consult anyone. I knew it was the right move. Have you ever known me not to know what I was doing?"

Mother shook her head dumbly.

"You've never made the decisions," Father went on. "I don't know why you should expect to start sharing in them now."

"You never *let* her make any decisions," said Nessie fiercely. "It's time you did!"

"Be quiet!"

It was the third time that Sunday morning that my father had used his tone of authority. Usually, if we irritated him to that degree, a hard day would follow. But he was excited, and little as he valued our opinions he wanted to show off his purchase.

"Anyway," he said, "we don't have to stand here and talk about it. Let's go inside." He produced a big heavy key from his pocket and threw open the front door with a flourish.

Ellen ran ahead of us through the big bare hall and in and out of the downstairs rooms. We heard her feet clattering around on the board floors. Geoff followed, and at once disappeared upstairs. Mother, Nessie, and I moved in more soberly, still shaken by the surprise that Father had sprung on us.

The house had been cleared completely. Not a relic remained of former occupation, nothing to indicate what kind of people had lived in it before. There was a total, echoing emptiness about it, as if it had been stripped not only of contents but of character—an empty vessel ready for a new use.

Father led us on a brisk tour, giving no time for more than a glance into the main rooms. There were four of these on each of two floors; they were large and high, but although the sun was shining outside, the light from the narrow windows was only moderate. The kitchen and bathroom were old-fashioned, and Mother grimaced at them, but Father hustled her past.

The view from the attics seemed to interest him more. The garden at the back was a good deal larger than that of the small modern house we were living in at present. There was an expanse of uncut shaggy grass, with a big unpruned apple tree in one corner. Round most of the grass were flower beds, half overrun by weeds, though a few tired end-of-season flowers still showed their heads. There were some straggly roses, though hardly enough to justify the name of the house. And beyond these was a fringe of big, well-established rhododendrons which had all grown together at the top but had a row of dark caves underneath. Over the tops of the rhododendrons you could glimpse the roof of a neighboring house, and over a high privet hedge at the side, the end wall of another. But these glimpses were no more than hints of the presence of other houses; it was obvious that even in winter you wouldn't see much of them.

"We're not overlooked, you see," said Father with satisfaction. "Nobody to take a nosy interest in what we're doing."

17

"What do we ever do to interest anybody?" Nessie whispered in my ear. Father glanced sharply at her but said nothing.

He seemed even more pleased by the cellars. "Plenty of storage there," he said. And then, to me, "You or Geoff can help me with a little job, Barry, before we go."

But Mother grew more and more unhappy as the tour continued. "This place still looks like a white elephant," she said when we'd finished. "And it must have cost an awful lot. And you always said you liked modern houses best."

Our other house didn't have either attics or cellars. It was semidetached and small, not to say poky; always neat and shipshape. "Just what we need and no more than we need," Father used to say. "No point in paying taxes on useless space."

But now, mysteriously, he seemed to have changed his tune.

"Things aren't as they used to be," he said. "An intelligent man can change his mind. An intelligent man adjusts to new circumstances."

Mother didn't say anything to that.

"As for the cost," Father said. "Well, it's certainly costing me a pretty penny. Five times what it would have done a year or two ago. But money's going down faster and faster. By next year it'll seem cheap. Dirt cheap."

"I'll feel lonely here during the day," Mother complained. "No neighbors nearby, and I don't know anybody around here anyway."

"Neighbors? I don't know why you bother about neighbors. Coming in, wasting time, drinking tea, borrowing things . . . You're better off without neighbors.

Anyway, I specially wanted a house with privacy. I have my reasons, May. Good reasons."

It was just as Father mentioned privacy that Geoff's voice came echoing down the staircase. He'd been up in the attics, looking out of the window.

"Dad!" he called. "Dad! There's somebody in the garden."

Father didn't like that at all. He stalked out to meet the intruder. The big untidy apple tree in the corner was laden with fruit, and more apples lay around it on the ground. A young man with long fair hair had found his way through the hedge and was now munching an apple. Father marched briskly up to him. The young man waited, quite at ease, and took another bite.

"This is a private garden," Father said stiffly.

The young man grinned amiably.

"Thought it was up for sale," he said.

"I'm the buyer."

The young man grinned again. "I'll take your word for it," he said.

"So the apples belong to me."

"OK, chief. You can spare a few, can't you?"

"That's not the point," Father said. "The point is that I'd prefer you to ask before helping yourself to my property."

"I'm asking you now. Look, I got a bag here, holds about a dozen. You don't mind, do you? The old lady likes a nice apple."

Father looked him up and down. Tall, very narrow hips, round face, blue eyes, cheerful unabashed expression.

"All right," he said shortly. "Just this once," and turned away. "May," he called to Mother, "find something to carry apples in. We're not wasting them."

He wasn't the only one who'd been looking the young man up and down. Nessie had been inspecting him, too; and he had noticed Nessie. Nessie was indeed noticeable in any company: taller than average, slim, with reddish-blond hair and wide, blue-gray eyes. Now, as Father's back turned, the young man winked at her. Nessie looked away but didn't seem offended.

"Hello," he said. "I'm Terry."

"Nessie!" Father called. "Come along!" And then, over his shoulder, to Terry, "You'd oblige me by going out through the gate, not through the hedge."

"We live just down the hill, in the old cottages," Terry said to Nessie. "Me and my mum. So we'll be neighbors, sort of. Well, not too far apart." He grinned engagingly.

Nessie didn't respond. But I thought I could interpret her expression. As we followed Father back to the house, I said, "Some interesting people around here, aren't there?"

"Are there?"

"He fancies you. Do you fancy him?"

"Mind your own business," said Nessie; but her lips twitched in the beginnings of a smile.

"I'll tell you one thing," Father was saying. "I'm going to put a stop to trespassing. That's something I won't have. It could spoil all my plans."

"What plans?" asked Nessie.

"Never you mind."

"Well now," Father said. "While your mother's fetching a bag to put those apples in, let's consider which rooms people are to have. It needn't take long, but I don't want any of you saying I haven't consulted you." He looked around at our faces. "Now, to begin with, the front bedroom obviously is for your mother and me. That's reasonable, isn't it? No questions there. Now, as for Nessie . . ."

"I don't mind about having a proper bedroom," Nessie said. "I'd like the front attic. I could play my records there and have friends in, and you wouldn't hear us."

"And I'd like the back attic," said Geoff. "Plenty of room there for my football gear. And my photography."

"Horrible noise," said Father automatically to Nessie; and, to Geoff, "Wish you'd take up a less expensive hobby." But he didn't seem to care a great deal. "Very well. That's all right. So Barry and Ellen can have the two middle bedrooms, and there's one to spare for guests."

"When do we have guests?" asked Nessie under her breath.

"And what about Cliff?" I inquired.

"Oh, about Clifford," my father said. "Well, I'm afraid Clifford won't be coming. He'll have to look for new lodgings."

Clifford was Father's assistant manager at the shop. He was in his early twenties: a smallish, thin, spectacled young man with a homely accent. When he came to the town a year earlier he hadn't anywhere to go, and he'd been given our tiny back bedroom "for the time being." But somehow or other he'd stayed. He was a quiet lodger who brought books home from the library and went to evening classes, no trouble to anyone. I got on rather well with him, and we often played chess.

"Did you say Cliff will have to look for somewhere else?" my mother said, coming in.

"That's right. He's had a good run. He always knew he couldn't stay with us forever."

"We had room for Cliff in the little house," Mother said thoughtfully, "but you say we're not going to have room for him in this great big one?"

"Correct."

"I wish I knew what you're up to, Norman. I just don't understand."

"There's a lot you don't understand, May. There always has been. I don't have to explain every move I make to you."

"I don't think Cliff will like to go," I said. "He doesn't have many friends. And . . ."

"And he won't like leaving Nessie!" finished Ellen.

"He wasn't getting anywhere, was he, Nessie?" Geoff asked.

"He certainly wasn't," Nessie said. "Poor Cliff. So shy he made even *me* feel embarrassed. If I spoke to him, he hadn't a word to say for himself."

"You must admit he's harmless," I pointed out.

Nessie smiled.

"Oh, yes, he's harmless. P'raps that's what's wrong with him. One of nature's harmless ones."

"Anyway, Clifford won't be coming here!" said my father with an air of finality. "And now, there's something else I have to do before we go. Barry, I want you to come down with me into the basement while the others collect those apples."

I followed him down the cellar steps, which led from the kitchen. Father had brought a tape measure. He kept me busy for several minutes, holding an end of the tape as he took various measurements. The basement was the full width of the house, with pillars helping to take the weight of the dividing walls above. Father made sounds of mild satisfaction as he jotted down figures in a notebook. He also remarked favorably on the absence of damp. Clearly he was still feeling pleased with himself.

"You're not taking any measurements in the house itself?" I asked him when he had finished.

"Eh? . . . Oh, no, that'll be all right. You lot and your mother can do anything that's needed. Now, just a minute while I look around outside."

Father turned his back on me to go into the garden, obviously not needing my company. I joined Geoff and Nessie, who had come in and were up in the attics again, planning where they would keep their possessions. But I didn't take much part in their talk. I was more and more puzzled by Father's enthusiasm for a house that he would formerly have dismissed as a white elephant, and by his strange interest in the basement.

I wandered across to the front attic window and looked down on his foreshortened figure as he walked a few paces across the gravel of the drive, his sharp black shadow stepping out ahead of him. He stopped, turned, and put a hand to his eyes against the sun, surveying the evergreens between house and road. Then he took out the notebook again and made what seemed to be a quick sketch.

Father was a compact, dapper man, a little below average height. His face was thin and tended toward sallowness. His eyes were blue and sharp; his hair had been fair but was graying now and thinning a little on the temples. As he moved around with his neat, slightly military step, making notes as he went, it struck me that he looked very much like an army officer surveying a position.

2

THE END OF NOVEMBER. Our third week in the new house. Fog all over the Midlands, and our city getting its share. Up on the Mount it was thin and drifting: only a blurring of lights, a slight taste in the mouth, an occasional ghostly effect as trees or houses appeared to glide into the mist and out of it again. Down in the city it was thicker. Nessie and I, late from school after a club meeting, walked with scarves round our mouths through the streets toward Father's shop; for it was closing time and we hoped for a ride home.

Father wasn't there, and most of the staff had gone, but we could see from the doorway that Clifford, his assistant, was at the till. And talking to Cliff was Stuart Hazell, who was in the top form at our school and hoping to go to university next year. They made an odd-looking pair; both were thin and wore spectacles, but Stuart, though five or six years younger than Cliff, was a head taller. Stuart was self-conscious about his height and was inclined to stoop, to bring himself down to other people's level.

"I don't want to talk to Cliff," said Nessie. "It makes me feel mean. He's so devoted, but I just can't feel anything for him. Come along, Barry—never mind getting a ride, let's walk."

But Cliff had seen us. He closed the till and came forward.

"Hello, Barry," he said. "Hello, Nessie. It's been a long time."

"How are your new lodgings, Cliff?" I asked.

"Not too good, really. Not as nice as being with your mum. But there you are, that's life."

"Mum misses you."

"I miss her. I miss you all." Cliff looked at Nessie, but she looked away.

"You haven't been to the new house, have you?" I said.

"Haven't been asked," said Cliff promptly.

"I should think something could be done about that," I said. "Where's Dad?"

"Went early."

"That's not like him," I said. "He always used to be here when the rest had gone."

"Your dad's changed lately," Cliff said. "At least, in some ways he's changed. Haven't you noticed?"

"He was never—well, ordinary," I said.

"I know that. But he acts as if he has something on his mind, something big. Does it seem so to you?"

"Well, yes. He spends a lot of time on his own, writing in notebooks or reading. And—"

"And he seems to be knocking the basement to bits," Nessie said. She had taken a model shoe out of the window and was contemplating it thoughtfully. "You haven't got much choice in the shop these days, have you, Cliff?"

"We have to take what we can get," Cliff said; and then,

reverting to his former subject, "It worries me a bit. Your dad's taking a lot of time off. And when he's here he isn't really here, if you know what I mean. I told him yesterday, the area manager's asked for him once or twice when he wasn't around. But it didn't seem to sink in."

"Will he get into trouble?"

"I shouldn't think so," Cliff said. "Of course, now the shop's part of a big chain, you can't be sure. But I don't think they'd like to lose your dad. He knows what's what in the shoe trade."

"Does it make more work for you, Cliff, when he's not here?"

"Oh, I don't mind a bit of extra work. It's all experience, isn't it? But things are difficult these days, with prices changing all the time."

"I'll say they're changing," said Nessie. She had another shoe in her hand now. "Thirty pounds for a pair of shoes! A year or two ago, I'd have expected a whole outfit for that."

Stuart had been listening in silence to the conversation so far. Now he said quietly, "Shoes are for the rich. Or soon will be."

There was a note in his voice that disconcerted me. Though Stuart was eighteen—two years older than I was—I knew him well. He had always been a mild, amiable person. But these words were said sharply, almost bitterly.

"What do you mean, Stuart?" I asked him.

"Don't you ever listen to the news?" Stuart said. "Don't you know we're in trouble? Don't you know nobody wants our money? Don't you know we have to import most of our food? Don't you know there's a crisis?"

"Oh, *that!*" I said. "There's always a crisis."

"This one's for real," Stuart said. "If you think things are dear now, just wait a few weeks. The scarcer they are, the dearer they'll get." His voice was rising. "And that goes for food, too. And when prices go through the roof, the rich and the strong will be all right, and the rest will go to the wall. And you know who those who go to the wall will be?"

He didn't wait for an answer.

"The poor and the old and the sick, that's who they'll be. And the government knows, and it doesn't care. Because what use are the poor and the old and the sick? They're not productive workers. They're not clever financial brains. It doesn't matter if they starve."

"Now, now, Stuart," Cliff said. "Calm down. It may never happen."

"It'll happen all right. And it matters to some of us. That's what we're forming Share Alike for."

"What's Share Alike?" inquired Nessie.

"It's what its name says. We'll try to see that everything's distributed fairly. We'll be a pressure group to start with. But if we don't get any response from the government, we may be forced to take things into our own hands."

Cliff pulled a disapproving face. Nessie had wandered to the other end of the shop and was fingering packets of tights on a rack.

"Maybe I ought to stock up on tights," she said thoughtfully. There was a self-mocking note in her voice which escaped the other two.

"Oh, well, I suppose you didn't come here for a lecture," Stuart said.

Cliff had been trying to get a word in. "Can I do anything for you?" he asked.

"I don't think so, Cliff," I said. "We thought Dad might have given us a lift home, that's all, but as he's gone already . . ."

"Oh, I can run you home," Cliff said. "I'll be ready in a minute. I'm just going to lock up."

"And I'm on my way, too," said Stuart. "And it doesn't matter if you forget what I say. Because you'll be reminded soon enough, by events. Good-bye."

Cliff stared after him as he stalked out of the shop. "He's a bit huffy," he remarked. "Mind you, I think he's right. But I don't like people talking about taking the law into their own hands. Now, I'll just go and bring my car round from the back."

"You needn't bother, Cliff," Nessie said. "We'd just as soon walk home."

"It's no trouble, Nessie," Cliff assured her. "No trouble at all."

Nessie said nothing, but gave me a quizzical look. "A bad case of D.D.," she said to me when Cliff had gone to fetch the car.

D.D. stood for dumb devotion, the quality in Cliff that particularly irritated Nessie. When he drove up, she got quickly into the back of the car, leaving me to sit beside Cliff in the front. But if Cliff was disappointed, he didn't give any sign of it.

"You'll have to show me the way," he said to me.

The fog was thickening, and it was dusk. I navigated with some difficulty as Cliff picked his way through the streets, looking for elusive turnings and sometimes getting them wrong. Up on the Mount, it was a little clearer.

Cliff drew up under a blurred street lamp outside our garden. "I'll drop you here and go on," he said.

That would have done very well for Nessie, but I didn't feel it was good enough when Cliff had been our lodger for more than a year.

"Come in and say hello to Mum," I suggested. So Cliff got out of the car and walked with us up the damp drive between gloomy evergreens.

"Nice place you have here," he said. "Big."

"Big's not the same as nice," said Nessie, making her first remark since we got into the car.

Then a group of children came round the side of the house toward us. There were four of them. Three were running rapidly and shrieking as they came. One lagged behind.

"Hurry up, Mel, he'll get you!" one of the leading children shouted back to the laggard.

I didn't think I knew any of the three who were in the lead, though in the misty dusk it was hard to be sure. They scattered and ran wide of us. But Mel, the fourth, wasn't in such a hurry. And I knew Mel. He was the son of Vince Holloway, of Holloway Projects Limited. Holloway Projects were anything that looked likely to make money, and Vince was supposed to be a smart operator. Mel was a smart operator, too, in a small way; he was a wizard at the kind of swapping and small trading that goes on endlessly among children. He was three or four years younger than I was—closer to Ellen's age than mine—and was dark, with a round, slightly goblinesque face and a perpetual grin, as if he were continually amused by his own cleverness. I didn't trust him an inch, but rather liked him.

I stretched my arms wide and Mel, without trying too hard to avoid me, ran into them.

"What's all this about, Mel?" I demanded.

"Oh, only your dad chasing us," said Mel, hardly out of breath and not much perturbed.

"Chasing you for what?" I asked.

"Don't ask *me*," said Mel. "We didn't do anything. Your Ellen invited some of us to come round. We were looking for the back door, that's all. And out he came." Mel raised his eyebrows comically. "Whew! Then the balloon went up!"

At that moment my father came round the side of the house. He was wearing overalls, not his usual neat dark suit. And he was walking fast, though not actually running.

"I saw you, Mel Holloway!" he shouted. "And the rest! Nosy-parkering around! I won't have it. I won't have it, I tell you!"

As Father approached, I let Mel go, because Father's explosions of temper could be fierce, and I didn't want him to lay hands on anyone. But Mel was not afraid at all, and stood his ground after I'd released him.

"We only came to play with Ellen," he said, his usual grin returning to his face. "We weren't doing any harm."

Father stared at him. I could feel the strain as he brought himself under control, like a heavy lorry braking hard. When he spoke, his voice was very quiet.

"All right, Mel Holloway," he said. "Get along with you now. Another time, if you are invited to this house—*if* you are invited to this house—you can come straight up the front drive to the front door and ring the bell. And stay there until somebody lets you in. You understand?"

"Yes. Sure, Mr. Mortimer," Mel said, unabashed.

"But just for now, Ellen doesn't want to see anybody. She doesn't need people coming around. She has her dog and her hobbies and the television. She's very fully occupied."

"Yes, Mr. Mortimer," Mel said. "So long, Mr. Mortimer. So long, all." And off he went, in no hurry, toward the front gate.

Father looked after him. I could still sense the tension, and was puzzled by it. But in Cliff's presence Father was taking pains not to let it show.

"It's good to see you here, Clifford," he said. "A pleasant surprise."

"Cliff ran us both home," I told him.

"Nice of him."

There was something dismissive in Father's tone, and Cliff recognized it. So did I, but I didn't want Cliff to go.

"I thought he'd like to have a talk with Mother," I said.

"Oh, yes. Yes, of course," said Father, though he didn't sound too pleased. "Well, come into the house, Clifford. Sit down in the lounge. I'll tell my wife you're here."

"I expect she's in the kitchen, isn't she?" Cliff said. "I'll just go through, like I always used to do. She won't expect me to stand on ceremony."

"Oh, you're a visitor now, not a lodger," Father said. "Visitors are treated properly in my house, not relegated to the kitchen." He headed Cliff off, and almost herded him into the big, high, drafty front sitting room. Ellen sat there on the sofa, huddled in a rug, watching television. Her black and tan mongrel, Peggy, lay on the sofa beside her. Father strode across the room, switched off the television, and put the dog on the floor.

31

"You can go to your room, young lady," he said. "I'll have a word with you later. About encouraging stray children to come hanging around the place."

"Oh, have they come?" Ellen asked, half eagerly, half apprehensively.

"They've come. And they've gone. And another time you'll tell me before you do anything like this. Now, off you go to your room. And Clifford, sit down, do. I'll just put this gas fire on for you."

The gas fire breathed out a little pink warmth, soon lost in the cavernous spaces of the room. Nessie, I noticed, had slipped quietly away. And when my mother came into the room, wiping her hands on her apron, Father wasn't with her.

Mother was usually undemonstrative, but she went straight to Cliff and put her arms round him.

"Cliff!" she said. "Cliff! We've missed you. I wish you could have come sooner."

"Cliff was pointing out just now," I said, "that he hasn't been asked."

"He shouldn't need to be asked," Mother said.

"Seems you do need to," said Cliff. "Those children weren't very welcome."

Mother sighed.

"I shouldn't speak out of place," she said. "But oh, dear, Father's difficult these days. And it's such a strain, living in this big cold house. It felt cold in here even before it started actually *being* cold. And now—well, it makes you shiver, doesn't it, Barry?"

"It makes me shiver in more ways than one," I said. "I just don't like it."

"I can't think why anybody should buy a house like this

32

unless they can afford to get it centrally heated," Mother said. "But Norman says we haven't the money for that. And look at the carpet in this room. It was wall-to-wall carpet in the little house we had before. Look at it now, with stretches of floorboard all around. Oh, we used to be so warm and comfortable, and now . . . But I suppose I mustn't complain."

"I don't see why you shouldn't complain," I said. "Especially when it's only to Cliff, who's like one of the family."

"Well, your father wouldn't like it," Mother said. "And he never could stand being crossed."

From somewhere below us came the sound of sawing.

"What *is* he up to?" I demanded.

"He's putting up a lot of shelves. Lots and lots of shelves. I don't know what for. He doesn't like me to go down there. Keeps it locked most of the time. He says we've got so much pantry space that I don't need to use the basement." Mother sighed. "The only person who's close to him now is Geoff."

"Is Geoff down there with him now?"

"I think so."

"Why should Geoff be the one to be close to him?" Cliff asked.

Mother looked at me.

"Oh, he's always preferred Geoff to me," I said. "I don't mind."

Nessie had come into the room. "You do mind," she said. "Of course you mind."

"Well, Geoff's more like Father's idea of what his son should be," I said. "Down-to-earth and practical, you know. And he enjoys helping Father and doing jobs and making things. At least, I suppose he enjoys it. He doesn't say much."

"Geoff never was talkative," Mother said.

"Anyway, Geoff's quite happy, so far as I can see," I said. "And you're all right, aren't you, Nessie? You're all right because you're never here."

"Where am I at this moment?" Nessie asked.

"Well, you're here just now. But you're not *often* here, are you?"

"Nessie has a new boyfriend," Mother said tactlessly. "His name's Terry. He's *very* good-looking."

"Oh!" said Cliff.

"And she seems to spend lots of time at his house, I don't know why."

"It's warm and cheerful, and people are nice there, that's why," said Nessie.

"But the rest of us are stuck," Mother said. "I don't even seem to get out to the shops anymore. Father's started doing all the shopping himself. . . ."

Then she fell silent. We heard Father's steps coming along the hall. It had always been the same in our household; Father's approach made us feel guilty, like naughty children awaiting a teacher who will find out their misdeeds. And Father had extraordinarily keen hearing. He was always likely to overhear just the one remark you didn't want him to catch. He did so now.

"What's that, May?" he said. "What's that about shopping?"

"I just said you'd started doing it," Mother said. And then, recklessly, "And if you want to know, I was going to say that I'd rather do it myself. After all, I always used to. And I managed, didn't I?"

"You managed at one time," Father said. "But now it's different. There are lots of problems, and they'll get worse. It takes a man's mind to sort them out. You just get on with your housework, May, and leave the rest to me."

"Do only men have minds?" asked Nessie, half under her breath. Father shot her a look but didn't say anything.

"I'm only a housekeeper," Mother complained.

"And what's wrong with that? I wish my life was as easy."

Mother said no more. There was a familiar look of resignation on her round, once-pretty face. Nessie and I had always supposed that Father married Mother for her looks. But Mother's looks weren't the kind that wore well. Probably, we thought, Father now saw her as an only moderately efficient employee who couldn't easily be dismissed.

Father turned to Cliff.

"Well, now, Clifford," he said. "As I say, it's good to see you. Nice of you to bring my youngsters home. I must say, children are getting spoiled these days, taken here, there, and everywhere by car. They'll be forgetting how to walk. When I was their age I went on Shanks's pony, and it never did me any harm. But thank you all the same, Clifford. Has anything happened at the shop since I left?"

"Not really, Mr. Mortimer. Had Head Office on the phone. We'll be putting new tickets on everything again on Monday."

"All going up, eh?" my father said. "Second time this month. Oh, well, we've had plenty of warning, haven't we?" He didn't look too worried. "And what about our wages?"

"They go up, too. First of next month, up twenty percent."

"None too soon," said Father. "And none too much. Oh, well. . . ." There was a pause. "I expect you'll want to be on your way now, Clifford, won't you?"

"He's not in all *that* much of a hurry, are you, Cliff?" my mother asked. But Cliff had taken the hint.

"Yes, time I was going, Mr. Mortimer."

"Cliff hasn't had a look round the new house," my mother pointed out. "And after all, he lived with us a long time. We ought to let him have a look."

"You heard what Clifford said, May," my father said. "It's time he was going, that's what he said. Don't force him to insist."

Nessie and I walked with Cliff down the front drive toward his car. Peggy came with us, skipping and frolicking. For the moment, the fog seemed to have cleared. As Cliff got into the car, Terry walked up the street. Without embarrassment he and Nessie put their arms round each other. Cliff switched on the car engine, then spoke to me through the partly open window, his voice inaudible at any distance over the engine noise.

"That's the new boyfriend, eh?"

I nodded.

"I can't compete with him," Cliff said ruefully. "Not on looks, anyway."

"He may not last," I said.

Cliff grinned. "I might not be able to compete with the

36

next one, either," he said with equal ruefulness, and let in the clutch.

I would have walked past Nessie and Terry, who were still embracing, but Nessie disengaged herself and said, "You know what, Barry? I reckon we need to find out what he's up to."

"Who? Father?"

"Yes, of course. Father. When I was out of the room a few minutes ago I noticed our car standing round at the side of the house, just by the area steps, and it was stacked high with boxes. And the trunk was tied open, and that was stacked with boxes, too. There's something going on that he didn't want those children to see, and that he didn't want Cliff to see, either. Listen, Barry. We want to know what he's doing in that basement. And soon."

3

EARLY DECEMBER. I looked from the window of the front attic, now Nessie's room. There had been white frost, but the traces were gone now, except for a glisten of moisture on the grass and a lingering bruise of morning footprints. Outside our garden and lower down the Mount the trees were leafless now, but at Rose Grove there wasn't much change; we still had our big ragged fringe of drooping-dark-leaved rhododendrons and the tall fence of firs that edged the drive and did their best to hide the house from the road.

Early December, early afternoon. A half holiday at our school, thanks to Mr. William Windle, the not-very-famous politician who'd recently presented prizes at our speech day and had asked on our behalf for this traditional privilege. ("It's an ill Windle," our witty English teacher said, "that blows nobody any good.") Geoff had praised the name of Windle, because the half day had allowed him to go to a football match that he particularly wanted to see. Ellen had been peevish because she was still in elementary school and Mr. Windle had done nothing for her. She was at school as usual.

"Who gave you permission to be in my room?" Nessie's

voice asked from behind me, but it was a teasing voice, not an aggrieved one. I hadn't heard her come in.

"It doesn't feel all that much like your room, Nessie," I said.

"It looks just like my room to me. Bed unmade and clothes on every possible surface."

"But—oh, I don't know what it is. It looks only half inhabited. Where's your record player?"

"I took it down to Terry's."

"You were going to bring friends around and play records."

"Bring friends here? You have to be joking." Nessie joined me at the window. "God, what a gloomy place. As if things weren't bad enough this winter, without having to live *here.*"

"You're not here often," I pointed out. "Where's Terry now?"

"At work, of course."

"And that's why you're here, not there."

"Could be."

"Has Dad said anything about the amount of time you spend at Terry's?"

"Yes."

"What did he say?"

"I'll give you three guesses."

"He said, 'You're too young to be serious.' "

"No."

"He said, 'Don't trust that young man. Make sure you're never alone in a room with him.' "

"No."

"He said, 'Watch out or you'll get yourself talked about.' "

"No."

"All right, I give up."

"He said, 'You needn't start bringing him home for meals every day. I've enough mouths to feed, without his.' "

"I don't like the sound of that," I said.

"Nor do I. He's developing some kind of obsession, I think. The funny thing is, he doesn't *intend* to drive me away. He just does it without intending."

We were still at the window. "Hey, Nessie," I said, "there's Mother, going out. I thought she never went out these days. At least, that's what she's always saying."

Mother was wearing a dark mackintosh and carrying a bulging shopping bag. She had Peggy with her on the lead. Her body was bent slightly forward, and there was an oddly furtive air about her.

"Going to Mrs. Armitage's, that's my guess," said Nessie.

"Mrs. Armitage? She lives back near the old house."

"There's a bus."

"But . . . Mother never says anything about seeing people."

"Barry, dear," said Nessie, "Mother never says anything about anything. But how do you think she's lived with Dad for twenty years? She has a secret life."

"She *what?*"

"Oh, I don't mean she has a moustachioed lover tucked away somewhere. But she has little bits of life of her own, hidden where Dad doesn't see them. Habits, interests, things, people she knows, places she goes to—not often, but when she can't stand it anymore."

"How do you know all this?"

"I know more than you think. Superior perception, that's what it is. Boys don't have the gift."

"I suppose not." I was chagrined. "I think I have a bit of it. You know what? I'm nearer to you than I am to Geoff. I'm not on Geoff's wavelength at all. He's closer to Dad."

"You don't understand Geoff," said Nessie.

"Well, they're together in what goes on in the basement," I said. And then we looked at each other.

"Barry, there's only us two in the house."

I knew what Nessie had in mind.

"Yes," I said. "We could go down there. That's if we can get in. You know he keeps both doors locked."

"I know where there's a key."

The basement had two doors. One, at the top of a flight of concrete steps, opened into the kitchen. The other opened into a half-below-ground area at the side of the house.

An old-fashioned laundry room also opened off the kitchen. It was still used more or less for its original purpose; at least, the washing machine and dryer were kept in it. Nessie led me into this room, put a hand into the narrow space between wall and washing machine, and groped. For a few seconds she looked anxious. Then a smile broke on her face, and she withdrew her hand holding a big old-fashioned key.

"This," she said, "is the key to the cellar. And it had better be back on its hook before long."

The key turned easily in the lock. We went together down the steps. For no reason at all, since there was no one in the house, we tiptoed and spoke in whispers to each other.

When we first looked into the basement, I blinked. I remembered it as large, but it seemed to have shrunk to the size of one of the rooms above. The walls were white. Against the farther one was a workbench, and there were also tools, garden equipment, battered pieces of clumsy old furniture, and various household items of the kind that are bulky and not very beautiful or used very often. If I hadn't been in the basement before, I'd have thought that was all there was.

"Well, I don't know what we were expecting," Nessie said, "but there doesn't seem to be anything."

"You didn't come down here when we were looking round the house, did you?" I asked.

"No. It's the first time I've been in the basement. We've been in the house for a month, but we haven't exactly been encouraged to come down here."

"Well, I've been here before," I said, "and it's not the same."

I walked over to the facing wall, and realized that it was only a painted, room-high partition. If you stepped behind a big old-fashioned wardrobe at one end of it, you could pass through an opening into a much larger area behind. I did so.

"Where are you?" Nessie called.

"Here. Come this way."

Nessie joined me. "You'd think it was meant to hide the way through," she remarked.

"Yes," I said. "You would. And I do."

My voice, raised slightly on the last two words, was edged with a faint echo. The cavernous area in front of us was dark except for a little feeble light that filtered through the single grimy pane of the half-below-ground window. As my eyes became used to the gloom I could see that there was also a horizontal pencil line of light at floor level close to that window—obviously indicating the door to the open air.

"What's he hiding?" Nessie said, still in a low voice.

"We'll have to see. I'll go for a flashlight." But as I turned, I saw that there was a light switch on the wall beside me. When I flicked it down, a single low-power bulb came on, leaving most of the place in shadow.

"Shelves!" Nessie said. "Racks. Yards and yards of them! *That's* what all the hammering was about!"

And indeed the alcoves formed by the brick pillars that held up the internal walls above had almost all been filled with broad shelving. There was an elusive, rather pleasant smell of raw new wood mixed with something else that I couldn't yet identify.

The shelves nearest to us were empty, but those toward the farther wall had something on them. Something bumpy, but you couldn't tell what, because it was covered with black polythene sheeting. The lowest shelves were at waist height, and under them were more humped, sinister-looking black polythene shapes. And there were bins—black plastic dustbins, from the look of them—and black-painted metal drums, and tea chests. There was something faintly menacing about the whole array.

Nessie shuddered.

"I don't like it," she said. "Let's get out of here."

But then we looked at each other, and she shook her head.

"No," she went on reluctantly. "We're here. We'd better look."

We went toward the nearest loaded shelf. The black polythene sheeting was tucked in at the edges under heavy, bulky objects. I drew it back unwillingly, apprehensively.

There were cans on this shelf. Great big cans—cans of coffee, cans of drinking chocolate, cans of peas and tomatoes, cans of soup base—cans with familiar labels that I'd seen again and again in the shops, but bigger, giving a curious and alarming impression that they'd grown, and might still be growing.

"They're like you get at the cash-and-carry," Nessie said.

I tucked the polythene back under the front row of cans, glad to get them out of sight. Below the shelf was a row of bins. I took the lid off the first. It held half a dozen big, clear plastic sacks. In the poor light I couldn't see what was in them. With an effort I heaved one out.

"Rice," said Nessie. "Twenty-eight pounds of rice."

"That's a lot of rice."

"A lot more when it's cooked," Nessie said.

I put it back. In the next bin was dried potato, in smaller sacks. In the next, dried fruit. In the next, a plastic sack of salt and a stack of packeted soups. I identified at last the light lingering smell that had puzzled my nostrils. It was the aroma of dry, mixed foods that you might find in an old-fashioned grocery store.

I passed over the next few bins. Beyond them was a mysterious stack entirely covered by black polythene and tied with cord. I left it alone. And in a corner were four big plastic drums. COOKING OIL, read the labels. TWENTY LITERS.

Nessie had her back to me now, examining another

waist-high shelf. I turned to see. This shelf held cases such as you sometimes saw empty at the back of the supermarket, but now full of cans. They were more ordinary-sized cans than the ones we'd looked at before—cans of stewed steak, cans of meatballs, cans of chopped ham and of corned beef, cans of sardines, cans of condensed milk. Cans by the dozen, cans by the score. Cans that were overwhelming—this time not because of their size but because of their sheer numbers, as if the place were infested with cans.

"I don't like it," Nessie said for the second time, and shuddered again. "It's uncanny."

The weak unintended pun sent us into disproportion-ate paroxysms of nervous laughter.

"Uncanny!" I gasped out. "That's just what it's not! It's the c-c-canniest place I've ever seen!"

Nessie burst into fresh laughter.

"I don't know what I'm laughing for," she said. "It's not funny." But she was laughing again already, and so was I.

That was why we didn't hear anyone approach, until suddenly the door from the open air was thrown wide and daylight poured in. And Father's voice in sudden strained fury shouted, "Who's there?"

Nessie and I were instantly silent. We weren't actually in his line of sight. We looked at each other, and made to creep back toward the partition we'd come around. But Father was much too quick for us. There was a scurry of footsteps and he was there, confronting us.

"So!" he said. "So!"

Nessie still held in her hand a corner of the polythene sheeting from the shelf we'd been looking at. She drew it slowly over the cases of cans and pushed it under the edges as if tucking them into bed. I cursed myself for not remembering that although it was only midafternoon Father couldn't be counted on these days to be at the shop.

"So!" said Father again, and paused.

I felt a twinge of fear at the base of my stomach. Down here, half underground, away from the world, it didn't feel safe to be facing Father, even though there were two of us. I had a sense of violence in the air.

But seconds passed, and the tension diminished. In the end Father said in a quiet voice, "I suppose it was bound to happen." Another pause. Then, "Geoff didn't tell you, did he?"

Nessie shook her head.

"Good lad," Father said, referring to Geoff. "Of course, I should have known he wouldn't." He was silent again. Then, "You're the two oldest," he said. "Sooner or later you'd have had to know. It had better be sooner. I hope I can trust you, that's all. Can I trust you? Can I trust you not to talk? To *anyone?*"

Nessie said, very slowly, "I don't know what it's about. I don't like making promises about things I don't understand."

For a moment there was an expression on Father's face of mixed hurt and anger. The sense of underlying violence flared, then died down again.

"Very well, Agnes," he said, in a carefully reasonable tone. "If you can't take what your father does on trust, I quite see that you will have to have an explanation."

He paused. The idea of giving us an explanation seemed to appeal to him more on further thought. He stood with his legs a little apart and hands clasped behind

46

his back, reminding me of a film shot I'd seen of an officer giving a talk to the men under him.

"Listen carefully, please," he said. "I don't want to have to repeat myself. . . . Now, you know about the difficulties that this country is in?"

I groaned. "Who doesn't?" I said.

"You think it's all a great bore, don't you? You think it's all been said before for as long as you can remember?" He didn't wait for any comment. "Well, this time you're wrong. This time the big trouble's coming. It's really on the way."

I recalled what Stuart Hazell had said in the shoe shop.

"You know about prices doubling in six months," Father said. "Well, that's nothing. Absolutely nothing. People haven't yet realized what they're in for. It won't be only doubled prices. I'm telling you that before long there'll be little enough to buy at *any* price. What do you do when you run out of cash and you still have to eat and you can't borrow any more?"

"Do you mean us?" Nessie asked. "A family?"

"A family or a whole country, the principle's the same. No cash, no credit. What do you do then? Tell me."

I was silent, not knowing any answer. And no doubt silence was what Father expected. But Nessie said thoughtfully, "You beg, or you steal."

"A good reply," said Father, surprised. "There are times, Agnes, when I think you ought to have been a man. You have the brains for it, or very nearly. However, a country can't beg. Or at least, it can, but there comes a time when people just won't hand out any more, and that's what's happened to us. And a country can't steal. Unless you think we can send an army to plunder other countries. And the days when we could do that are gone. So *now* tell me what happens."

This time neither Nessie nor I had anything to say.

"I'll tell you," Father said. "You collapse. You go to the wall. Because there isn't anywhere else to go."

"Thank you for cheering us up," said Nessie.

"However, a moment ago you talked of the family. Now, for a family it's not quite the same. There's one thing a family can be. Or rather, there's one thing the head of a family can be. The head of a family can be prepared. This is a time—I hope you're still listening carefully—this is a time for being prepared. And I'm prepared."

A note of satisfaction was beginning to creep into Father's voice.

"Education's a very fine thing," he said, "and I never had any worth speaking of. But the educated don't have a monopoly of brains. Do they? Do *you* think the educated have a monopoly of brains, Barry?"

"No," I said.

"No, of course not. Mind you, they can keep you down if you don't have education. They can keep you down in an ordinary job, far below your abilities. Oh, yes, they can do that. I know it, to my cost. But there are times when brains will out. And this is one of them. I can see as far into the fog as any educated man, and farther than most. And I can see what's going to happen. Soaring prices—we're getting those already—and then the time when nobody wants money at all and there's nothing to be got."

I remembered Stuart again.

"And those who suffer," I said, "are the old and the poor and the sick."

"That's right," Father said. "They'll be the principal sufferers, I dare say. But not the only ones. We'll all be at risk. And *we* don't want to suffer the same as them, do we?"

He leaned forward.

"I'll tell you something," he said. "I've made a resolve. I've resolved that, come what may, my family are not going to the wall. I grew up in a hard school, you know. I grew up in the Depression. And I was let down by my dad. He had a small business and drank the profits. Did nothing for us. No education for us, there wasn't, and education didn't grow on trees in those days. But do you think I'll let you down as my dad let me down? Oh, no. I'll see you through. I'll see every one of you through. If disaster comes, it won't come to *us.*"

Father was beginning to sound almost excited.

"I take it as a challenge, you see," he went on. "A challenge I'll meet head-on and beat. A challenge, you could almost say, that I've been waiting for. There are times that show what a man's really made of, and I reckon we're coming up to one of them."

He turned to the nearest stack and drew back the polythene with an air of pride, as though it were an unveiling.

"Stores!" he said. "That's the key to the situation. Stores!"

Nessie, standing beside me, had been staring at Father as he spoke. In the poor light I couldn't decipher her expression. Now she said softly into my ear, as if she couldn't hold the words in any longer, "It's sick-making!"

"Eh? What did you say?" Father asked. But he didn't stop to press for an answer.

"You know what?" he said. "I reckon that in a few

months' time there'll be folk coming *crawling* for a bit of what we've got. *Crawling.*" The word obviously gave him pleasure. "At least, they would if they knew. But they'd better not know, had they?"

I felt oddly divided in my mind. I knew just how Nessie felt. But there was a part of me that found a kind of shameful comfort in the thought of all those supplies. Food was solid and real and sustaining, and the time might come when we'd be glad of it.

And the thought was also in my mind that this wasn't the moment for the row that was lying around, waiting to happen, between Nessie and Father.

"There must be enough here to last us for a long time," I said, for the sake of keeping the talk going and keeping Nessie out of it.

"Six months, I reckon, already," said Father. "But I'm preparing for a long war—I mean a long crisis. I'd like to be set up for two years. And we can't lose by it, Barry. You realize that? We can't lose by it. Even if things don't get as bad as I expect, food will still keep going up and up. We'll be sitting on a little gold mine."

He moved along the racks, almost as if conducting a guided tour.

"It takes thought," he said, "to plan an operation like this. Of course, I had the advantage of being a quartermaster, once, in army days. And you have to make use of your advantages, especially if you never had many of them. Anyone might think of buying rice and a few cans, but not everyone would think of the things *I* think of. Look there. Lentils. Very rich in protein, very economical in space. Meat extract in big jars. Same again. Peanut butter, same again. And those boxes over there are dried fruit. Very concentrated, that. A little goes a long way. And golden syrup. And dried peas, dried onion, dried egg . . ."

"Oh, marvelous!" said Nessie; and I hoped that only I caught the note of irony.

"That's a whacking great deep freeze you have over there, too," I said.

"Yes. We'll have fresh meat for as long as we can. It probably won't be forever. And over in that corner, you see, there's a generator. That'll run the deep freeze and a few other things as well if the power fails."

"You really have thought of everything, haven't you?"

"Just about everything, I think," said Father. "And it's not only food you need, to keep going for a long time. Soap, for instance. Those boxes over there are full of soap. Not your fancy scented stuff. Real soap, carbolic soap. And soap powder for washing clothes, and polish, and brushes. And toothpaste, and plasters, and bandage, and disinfectant. And water purifying tablets, because we don't know what might happen to water supplies. We can always get water somewhere, but we don't know what *kind* of water. And just come along here. Batteries, oil lamps, candles. And those big drums are kerosine . . ."

"It's like Noah's Ark," said Nessie. "All we need are the animals."

"Noah's Castle," I said without thinking.

Father caught the phrase and seemed pleased by it.

"Noah's Castle," he said. "Not bad. I suppose it should be Norman's Castle really, seeing that's my name, but Noah's Castle sounds better. Noah's Castle. Yes, very good. And Noah won out in the end, didn't he? The rest got drowned, but not old Noah. He was prepared, like me."

There was a satisfied expression on Father's face.

"And I've got things he wouldn't have dreamed of. You can bet your boots he didn't have dried milk or concentrated orange juice or macaroni. And I've got brandy and whisky—not to drink, but they might come in handy for swapping. And cigarettes, too. I hate the things myself. Bad for your health. But I remember in the war the lads who went abroad often found them useful for buying things with when money wasn't wanted. And there's one more thing I've got which is very important. I bet you can't guess what it is."

Nessie and I shook our heads.

"It's an inventory, a proper inventory. I know everything I've got and exactly where it is. It's all written down in my little book in that desk." He indicated a battered desk which had been in the sitting room in the old house. "I wasn't a quartermaster for nothing," he said. "No slipshod methods for me. I believe in keeping proper records . . . What's that noise?"

There was a clatter of footsteps on the cellar stairs.

"It's all right, it's only Geoff," said Father. "Well, Geoff, how did the match go?"

"Losing four-one when I left," said Geoff in tones of disgust. "I didn't stay to the end. Reckoned I might as well be making myself useful here."

"Good lad," said Father.

Geoff looked dubiously at Nessie and myself. He was solidly built, with a squarish, strong-jawed face, and was already taller and broader than I was, although a year younger.

"I thought Nessie and Barry weren't supposed to know about all this," he said.

"They had to know sooner or later," said Father.

"So I can tell them about things now?"

"Tell them anything you like," Father said. "I've decided to take them fully into my confidence."

"Oh," said Geoff. Then, "I bet they've no idea how much work there was to do." He seemed to brighten a little at the prospect of telling us about it. "Take those racks for a start. Dad and me made all those and put them up. Drew up a cutting list, brought the wood home, sawed it, assembled it, drilled the walls . . ."

"Oh, great," said Nessie dryly.

"And it was tricky doing those corners, I can tell you. And we made that partition. Looks just like a fixed wall, doesn't it, until you get close up to it. And we installed the generator. That was quite a job. The exhaust had to go out into the open. And I helped Dad bring all the stuff from the supermarkets and the cash-and-carries. So one way and another I think I've done quite a bit of work."

"You certainly have," said Father. "I couldn't have managed without you."

"Is there anything that needs doing now?"

"Well, there's some more stuff in the car to unload. But no hurry about that."

"I could watch the football results on television first?"

"Of course you could. Off you go. Tell me if there's anything interesting."

Father looked thoughtfully after Geoff's retreating back.

"He's grown so big I sometimes forget he's still only a

lad," he said. "Still keen on his football and his camera stuff and all that. But I'm proud of him."

Surprisingly, I found myself jealous of Geoff's standing with Father.

"Why did you ask him to help you?" I wanted to know. "Why him and not me?"

"A lot of good *you'd* be at putting up shelves!"

That hurt and silenced me, but Nessie said quietly, "It's not as simple as that. Somebody older than Geoff might have had doubts and asked questions. Geoff hasn't reached that stage—yet."

"Geoff appreciates his dad," said Father, "which is more than others always do." He paused, then added with a note of surprised respect, "Still, Agnes, that was a thoughtful remark of yours. When youngsters start to grow up these days, they get strange ideas. Notions about helping others and all that. They haven't the experience to know that it's all very well helping others, but nobody's going to help *you*. They don't understand about looking after Number One. They don't know what the world's really like."

"Cliff believes in helping others," I said, "and he's not a youngster anymore."

"Cliff's old enough to know better," said Father disapprovingly. "Perhaps you understand now why I didn't feel we could still have him as a lodger. He has an outsize conscience, that's his trouble. He'd keep tripping over it. I don't feel I could really trust him. Anyway, there are some things that need to be kept in the family, and this is one of them."

"You didn't feel you could trust *us* until a few minutes ago, did you?" Nessie asked.

"You're getting so sharp you'll be cutting yourself," Father said. "All right, I admit, I did wonder. But when it comes to the pinch, I expect you're as loyal as Geoff, both of you. I always knew I'd have to trust you in the end, and I do trust you."

"It's not entirely a matter of loyalty," Nessie said.

"Isn't it? I think it is. I think it's very simple. I think what it amounts to is that you and Barry won't tell anyone about all this, because if you did you'd cause trouble for your father. And you wouldn't want to do that, would you, Agnes?"

Nessie said, in a low, reluctant voice, "No."

"Or you, Barry?"

"No."

"So I shall take that as a promise of silence. Right?"

"We haven't promised anything," Nessie said.

"I think you have," said Father. He stamped his feet. "Getting cold down here, isn't it? Now we've got everything sorted out, let's go up into the warm."

"I'm going out soon," Nessie said.

"To Terry's, I suppose. I don't know what you see in that young fellow. He's likable enough, but he'll never get anywhere in the world. I wish you'd think seriously about the kind of young man you should encourage."

"Don't push it too far," said Nessie.

"What?"

"Oh, nothing."

I noticed as we went through the kitchen that Mother had come back, quietly and unobserved. She made no comment on our emergence from the basement, and Father, as usual, said nothing to her.

In the sitting room it wasn't much less chilly than down

below. The gas fire still breathed a faint pinky glow. Ellen, on the sofa, had a coat pulled round her shoulders as she watched television. She was small and thin for her age, with a pale, wistful face, and was always apt to feel the cold. Peggy sat beside her on the sofa, but on seeing Father removed herself promptly and slunk round to the back of it.

The football results were over, and Geoff had gone to change his clothes. It was a ministerial broadcast now: an appeal for hard work, public spirit, and national unity in the face of the gravest peril. The same boring stuff as for weeks and months past. The broadcast finished with a plea for restraint in trying to buy scarce goods, an assurance that there was enough of all kinds of food to go round if people would buy only what they needed, and a warning that if they didn't there would soon have to be rationing. After this Ellen switched over to a cartoon program, and Father didn't stop her.

"It's as well I made an early start with my stocking up," he said quietly under cover of the noise. "Buying's not so easy now, with all the tightening up there's been. They look askance at you in shops if you ask for two tins of anything, never mind a whole case. But I'm still getting what I can. I might try that supermarket down the hill tomorrow. Doesn't do to get too well known at any of them."

Peggy came out from behind the sofa, tail wagging ingratiatingly. Father didn't respond. There was a speculative look in his eye.

"We were talking about old Noah just now," he said. "Well, Noah took animals. He had a reason to. But I don't know what reason *I* have. Seems to me this is no time to be using up food and money on a dog."

The cartoon stopped as he was speaking, and the last few words fell clearly into the silence. Ellen jumped up.

"What do you mean?" she demanded.

"Nothing, nothing," Father said.

"Peggy doesn't eat much," said Ellen. "We couldn't do without Peggy."

"All right, I heard you," said Father.

4

MID-JANUARY. It was a cold, gray, ironbound January
—the kind of midwinter month when pavements and
lawns and gravel alike seem jarringly hard underfoot,
and there's no give in anything. But it was dry: no snow
and not much rain. Talk among the grownups was the
usual kind of talk, but much more anxious. Prices were
still soaring. ("It's no lark," said our witty English
teacher.) Everything now cost five times what it had the
previous summer, and the tickets in the shop windows
seemed to change almost weekly.

It seems odd now, but for a long time the realities
behind the talk and the figures didn't sink in. People who
were in work—like Father—had their wages increased
regularly, and although they never quite caught up
with prices they weren't in serious trouble. The
newspapers—themselves grown thin—were full of
stories about the hardships of the unemployed and of old
people on fixed incomes; but then, there hadn't been a
time in years when the papers didn't carry stories about
old people's hardships, and the few old people we actually knew seemed to have relatives and savings and
weren't really in great difficulty.

Cliff Trent could have told us of some very different cases, but Cliff was out of favor with my father and we hardly saw him. He had gone over Father's head to the area manager, and had been given time off every day to help the local voluntary services, now trying desperately to keep meal centers open for those old people who could get to them, and meals-on-wheels services for those who couldn't.

Father complained bitterly to Mother and me about both Cliff and the area manager. "Their loyalty should be to the firm," he said. "Of course, in the old days it would have been. It's not the same since the chain took over." And then, "I'm going to miss Cliff when he isn't there. Whatever his faults, Cliff's reliable, and I can go away and leave him in charge. But with both him and me away, there'd be nobody around but a lot of silly girls."

"You always used to be at work all day until we moved here," Mother pointed out.

"That was before the present crisis. Now I have the shopping to do."

"It was you who insisted on doing it," Mother said. The point was still a sore one with her. "I sometimes wonder what I'm *for*. Just cooking and cleaning, I suppose. I might as well be a servant."

"A servant would need wages," Father said—unaware, I was sure, of any cruelty in the remark.

Father in fact was still managing to spend a good deal of time in buying stores. He ranged over wide areas, picking up the odd can here, the odd packet there. At least once a week the car would draw up near the side entrance to the basement, and Father and Geoff would unload whatever Father had acquired. Rationing hadn't come in as yet, but there was a pretty effective form of rationing that consisted of largely empty shelves in the shops and extremely high prices for what little there was. Father was now paying more and more for what he bought, but still he went on. "While ever there's anything to get, and while ever there's a drop of petrol to bring it home with—which won't be for long, I may say—I'll go on stocking up," he told me once. Several sacks of cement and an assortment of timber also found their way into the basement. One day a large load of sand was delivered, supposedly to make a sandbox for Ellen; but Ellen had grown out of playing in the sand, and it lay in the garden under a tarpaulin, unused.

The stacks of food in the basement grew. And as they grew, Father became more and more careful in using them. Rations were doled out day by day to Mother to prepare. There was always enough to eat, but never too much. Father would spend most of his evenings in the basement, checking and listing and rearranging, coming out only for the television news.

Sometimes Geoff would help him with his self-imposed tasks, treating them apparently as a game that he was privileged to play with his father, but other times even Geoff got bored and went off to his photography or to watch sports on television. Though nothing had been said, Geoff seemed to have realized that Nessie and I—especially Nessie—felt uncomfortable about Father's activities; and he tended to sidle past us without speaking.

Nobody ever came to the house.

In one way, Nessie was glad of Father's obsession. It prevented him from paying much attention to Terry. In the past he had watched jealously over her movements. Now he seemed not to care. But when Nessie, pushing her luck a little and trying to find out whether Father's previous reactions had changed, proposed to invite Terry to supper, there were immediate objections.

"We're not feeding *him*," Father said. "Hasn't he a home? Can't he invite *you* to supper?"

"Terry's mother's a widow," Nessie said. "She's hard up. She hasn't got much. It's difficult for them to keep going at all, the way things are. Whereas *we* . . ."

"We what?"

"Well, we . . . we've got plenty, haven't we?"

"Oh. Have we? Nobody knows what our needs might be."

"It feels to me as if, whatever happens, we'll be all right."

"You keep your 'all right' feelings to yourself, my girl," Father said. "Yes, as a matter of fact we may be all right, just about, if we're careful. But never tell anyone that, *anyone*, do you hear me?" A note of suspicion came into his voice. "Have you said anything to Terry?"

"No," said Nessie, and added under her breath, "I'd be ashamed."

Father either didn't hear or chose not to hear.

"I remember you saying," he went on, "that when there's no other way of getting things, you beg or steal. Well, the less people know, the less likely we are to have things stolen."

"Terry's not like that!" said Nessie indignantly.

"*Anybody* might be like that if things got tough enough. And as for begging, remember, we've nothing to give away. We keep what we have for ourselves."

61

Father didn't feel the same about Mr. Gerald, though. He was delighted when a letter came to say that Mr. Gerald Bowling would be in our city next week and proposed to give himself the pleasure of calling on us.

Mr. Gerald was the younger of the two Bowling brothers who had owned Father's shop until they sold out to a chain store. Father was convinced that if they'd stayed they would have recognized his abilities and put him on the board. Mr. Gerald indeed had said as much; but that was after the Bowlings had sold out and weren't in a position to do anything about it.

After some thinking aloud about whether he and Mr. Gerald should dine in splendor on their own, Father invited Mr. Gerald to the family supper table. He was a well-preserved, rosy-faced man in his fifties, with crisp, slightly curly gray hair. "A real gentleman," Father told us. "One of the old school."

Father had allotted a bottle of wine to this occasion, and provided Mother with the ingredients for an excellent meal. Mr. Gerald expressed admiration.

"I don't know how you do it, Mortimer," he said. "Or rather, Norman. I hope I can call you Norman, now we're on purely social terms. I don't think I've had so good a dinner in a private house since I lost my poor wife, and that was two years ago."

"Thank you, Mr. Gerald," said Father.

"Just Gerald, please. As I say, I don't know how you do it. And in these hard times, too. My housekeeper and I eat very simply, and are thankful to eat at all."

Father looked surprised at that.

"You realize, Norman, the money that Edward and I were paid for the store has dwindled in value, dwindled sadly." Mr. Gerald sighed. "A splendid wine, this, if I may say so." He looked and sounded like a pleasant if somewhat melancholy gentleman. A gentleman of the old school, as Father had said. But suddenly the feeling came over me that Mr. Gerald was well aware of the impression he gave, and was consciously keeping it up. I wondered whether even the accent was quite his natural one. And although his air was relaxed and meditative, his eyes were sharp.

I noticed, among other things, that those eyes were taking good notice of Nessie.

Nessie in fact looked bright and excited, because she was about to go out with Terry. Father, not anxious to keep the womenfolk in the conversation, hadn't made any objection when told that she planned to leave as soon as the meal was over.

"An uncommonly pretty girl, your elder daughter," Mr. Gerald remarked when she'd gone.

"Yes, I think she's quite a credit to me," Father said.

"Seventeen, I think you told me. A nice age to be. I wish *I* were seventeen. She's still at school, I believe. What does she plan to do afterward?"

"Oh, secretarial work, if I have any say in the matter. Something to see her through until she marries."

"And I don't suppose *that* will be long," said Mr. Gerald. "Whoever she marries will be a lucky man. I expect she has plenty of admirers in tow."

"There's one at the moment," Father said. "I can't say I'm keen on him, though. One of these long-haired young chaps with no manners. I reckon she could do better."

"I'm sure she could," said Mr. Gerald. And then, reverting to the earlier subject, "How *do* you do it, Norman? So excellent a meal in such difficult circumstances."

"We don't always have meals like this," Father said cautiously. "Not by any means. But I admit, I've used a bit of forethought."

"A bit of forethought," Mr. Gerald repeated. "Yes, Norman, I'm sure you have. Yes, that would be characteristic of you." The expression was pleasant, but the eyes as sharp as ever. "I shall be in the city again, early next month. I wonder if I could possibly inflict myself on you once more. Or would that be an imposition?"

"I'd like nothing better," Father said.

"And we need some dog food," said Mother. Father was making up the list for the week's shopping.

"Dog food? Since when did we buy dog food?"

"I've always bought dog food," Mother said. "There were a few cans in the pantry when you took over the shopping, and I've been using those. But now we need some more."

"And what does dog food cost?"

"It was ten pounds a can last time I bought it. That was over a month ago. It'll be more now."

"You can bet it will. Twenty, I should think. It's ridiculous, May. Can't the dog eat scraps?"

"A dog Peggy's size can't live on scraps."

"It had better learn to," said Father. "Because it's getting no canned stuff while I'm in charge of the shopping. Which is as far ahead as I can see."

Then he looked down at Peggy, asleep on the kitchen floor.

"You're quite right," he said slowly. "That dog can't

really live on scraps. Therefore, whatever it eats will be taken out of our mouths, one way or another. And in the time that's ahead of us, that won't do."

"Aren't the times bad enough?" my mother asked.

"You've seen nothing yet," said Father.

Later that day I heard Father on the telephone. I wasn't deliberately trying to overhear him, but Father never bothered to keep his voice down, and I couldn't miss it.

"That's correct," he was saying. "It's a mongrel brought in from the streets. A stray, originally. We've looked after it for a while, but we can't continue. . . . Yes, I quite realize you're getting a great many such requests these days. . . . Understandable. . . . Yes, thank you very much, I'll bring it in on Wednesday morning."

I walked quietly away.

"It's Peggy's death warrant," I said. All of us except Father and Geoff— busy in the basement—were sitting in the kitchen, the one part of the house that was warm. Terry had come to take Nessie out, but had been persuaded to stay for a few minutes.

Peggy herself lay sprawled as usual on the kitchen floor. Terry tapped her in the ribs with his foot; you couldn't have called it a kick. She opened her eyes briefly, then closed them again. "You hear that?" Terry said to her. "You're for it." Peggy, without otherwise stirring, wagged her tail.

Ellen, playing some solitary game with her dolls in a corner, hadn't seemed to be taking notice. Now she said, incredulously, "You mean Dad's going to have Peggy *put down?*"

"I'm afraid so," I said.

"But he can't! I won't let him!"

"How will you stop him?" I asked.

"She isn't his to do away with. Peggy's *my* dog. I won't let her go."

"She won't be anybody's dog after Wednesday," I said, "unless we do something about it."

"Well, then," Nessie said, "what *are* we going to do about it?"

"It's no good arguing with your dad," my mother said flatly. "Once he gets it into his head that he's not going to keep a dog any longer, that's that. He won't change his mind." And then she went on, with unexpected spirit, "We'll have to get Peggy away from here, that's all."

"Where to?" I asked.

"She could come and live with me and the old lady," Terry said. "You like me, don't you Peggy? I'm your favorite human, aren't I?"

Peggy's tail wagged again. Ellen looked hurt, but managed not to say anything. Terry noticed, and added, "Your favorite human except Ellen."

"Could you really have her?" Nessie asked.

"Well, there's a problem. Trouble is, we can only just feed ourselves, never mind a dog. My mum's pension goes nowhere these days, and my wages not much further."

My mother said, "I could find food for a dog, you know." There was an expression almost of cunning on her usually guileless face. An image came to my mind of her going out of the house a few weeks ago with a bulging shopping bag. I wondered whether she had become skillful over the years at small deceptions and embezzlements. "Leave that part to me," she went on now. "I'd see that Peggy didn't come to any harm that way. Take her, Terry, if you can."

Ellen, tears in her eyes, bent forward over Peggy.

"It's for the best, love," my mother told her.

"But what," said Nessie, "will you tell Dad?"

"Nothing," Mother said.

"And when he asks where Peggy is?"

"I'll say nobody's seen her today."

"You think he won't guess?" I asked.

"He won't just guess," my mother said. "He'll *know* we've found somewhere for her."

"And then what will he do?"

My mother looked into my eyes. "He won't beat me," she said. "And apart from that, there's nothing he can do to me that he hasn't done already. I haven't anything to lose. . . . Ellen, love, where are you going?"

Ellen, eyes full of tears for her dog, didn't answer, but fled silently from the room.

"We'd better look for her," Nessie said. "There's no telling what she might take it into her head to do."

It took a worrying half hour to find Ellen. We discovered her at last in the spare bedroom—a room so spare that it was almost forgotten. Even then we might have missed her if we hadn't heard a movement in the big built-in wardrobe which was the room's only furnishing apart from a bed. Nessie flung the door open, and there she was.

"You're a silly girl," Nessie began. "You might have got shut in, and what do you think . . .?" Then she stopped, and we all looked at the clothes that were hanging in the wardrobe and lying folded on the shelves.

"They must be for me," Ellen said.

"Well, they won't fit anyone else, that's for sure."

Ellen held a white cotton vest up against herself.

"It's too big," she said. She took out another. "And that's even bigger."

Nessie took a dress from a hanger. "It's Ellen-size," she said. "It certainly wouldn't fit Mother or me. To say nothing of being something I wouldn't be seen dead in."

Ellen held the dress up in its turn. "This is far too big, too," she said.

"Dad thinks ahead," I remarked.

"My goodness, you can say that again." Nessie was working her way through the wardrobe now. There were vests, pants, skirts, blouses, dresses, pullovers—all of stout manufacture and staid design, and all by varying amounts too large for Ellen.

Terry stared.

"What's it all about?" he demanded.

"Just that Dad thinks there are going to be shortages," Nessie said in a casual tone. "It looks as if he's bought some things for Ellen to grow into."

"Oh," said Terry. He turned to Ellen. "You know what, kid? Your dad cares about you. He does. He really cares."

"If he cared about me, he'd care about my dog," said Ellen.

"That's not the way he looks at it," said Nessie.

Ellen didn't want to see Peggy leave the house. She went to bed, still tearful. Nessie, Terry, and I set out with Peggy on the lead while Father was watching the television news. Mother slipped a newspaper-covered package into my hand which I took to hold Peggy's initial rations.

"You haven't met the old lady, have you, Barry?"

Terry asked as we walked between the evergreens down the drive from our house.

"No. I hope she'll like me."

"Oh, don't worry. She'll like you. She likes everybody. That's her trouble. Can't cure her of it."

Terry and his mother lived in one of four or five rows of houses, built as workmen's dwellings, that clung to the lower slopes of the Mount. "Sliding down into town," Terry said.

Mrs. Timpson let us into a tiny living room. Surprisingly, though fuel was scarce and dear, the room was cozy.

"What a lovely log fire!" Nessie said, embracing her.

Mrs. Timpson hugged us in turn and patted Peggy on the head. She was a small, dumpy, smiling woman who looked a little older than Mother.

"Terry brought home the logs," she said.

"Best not say too much about that," Terry warned her.

"Go on, tell," said Nessie.

"I found wood in the gardens of the big houses up on the Mount. Could even be that some of it came from *your* garden. Well, it wasn't being used, was it?"

"You'd better watch it if you come wood-gathering in my dad's garden," I said. "Your name'll be mud with him, to say the least."

"It's not much better than that now," said Terry. And then, "Hey, Mum, we brought you something."

"Good. What?"

"You're stroking it now."

"What d'you mean, Terry?"

"A dog. We brought you a dog. Name of Peggy. Surplus to requirements at previous establishment."

"What would I want a dog for?"

"Company."

"I've got you, haven't I?"

"Ah, yes, but a dog stays at home more."

"You have a point there." Mrs. Timpson and Peggy were fussing happily over each other. "But you're not serious, are you? You're not telling me that somebody's trying to give me this dog?"

"No. Only lend it you," said Terry. "She's Ellen's dog, really. But if she doesn't find a home, she's for the high jump."

"There's lots of dogs being put down these days," said Mrs. Timpson, "with food so scarce."

"She'll get food parcels," Terry said.

Nessie intervened. "You don't have to have her," she said. "Don't let Terry overpersuade you. It's a lot to ask."

"You shut up, Nessie," said Terry. "It's all over bar shouting. A dog was just what you wanted, wasn't it, Mum?"

"Well. . . ."

" 'Course it was."

"Well, I suppose it *would* be company."

" 'Course it would."

"I'll think about it. . . . Now, it's a cold night. How about a baked potato each? They'll bake beautifully in these ashes. Do you both like baked potatoes?"

"You'd better," said Terry. "Because there's nothing else."

"At least there's plenty of these," said Mrs. Timpson.

"We both love them," Nessie said.

Terry was down on his knees, fighting a mock battle with Peggy. She growled at him and he growled back. "Don't get fierce," he told her. "You got yourself a home, Peggy. Not as posh as the other, but a home."

"Who says?" asked Mrs. Timpson.

"I say."

"Oh, well, maybe we can see how we get on. At least she won't give me the cheek you do."

Terry winked at us. "What did I tell you?" he said.

"He twists me round his little finger," Mrs. Timpson complained. "Now shift yourself out of the way, Terry, and let me get to the fire with these potatoes."

As it turned out, Father didn't make a fuss over the disappearance of Peggy. I was sure that Mother was right; he knew perfectly well that she'd been spirited away, but his object had been achieved, and he was satisfied. "So long as we're not feeding that animal, I don't mind," he said, having asked a few questions and received evasive answers. "But I don't want to see any food going out of here."

Father had a bigger problem on his mind than Peggy. His staff at the shop was being cut back. There were no longer the shoes to sell. He explained matters to me one evening after a particularly gloomy television news bulletin. Mother and Ellen were in the kitchen, Nessie out, and Geoff in his room. According to Father, the management of the shoe shop chain kept putting their prices up and up, but by the time the shoes were sold and the money from selling them was used to produce more shoes, it wasn't enough, because production costs had risen still further in the meantime.

"In fact, they're losing interest in selling shoes for paper money at all. Paper's no good to them. What they'd really like to do is export all they make and get Swiss francs for them. Swiss francs and gold are the only things that mean anything now."

"They won't close the shop, will they?" I asked.

"I don't think so. They can find the paper money to pay me and Clifford with, and I suppose they think things will get back to normal someday and they'll still want to be in business. Someday! It could be a long time till someday!"

"I've been thinking about it, you know," I said.

"Well, that's interesting. I'm glad to see those brains of yours being put to some use. I thought I was the only one who ever bothered to think around here."

"I'd like to ask you something."

"Ask away," said Father; but he stiffened all the same. He had never liked being questioned.

"I wonder how you've managed to pay for all the things you've bought in the last few months," I said. "They must have cost a fortune."

My heart thumped. I thought Father might be furious. But to my surprise he smiled.

"Well, now you *are* asking," he said. "And I'll tell you. But listen, Barry, no passing this on to your mother and sister, eh? It isn't women's stuff, this isn't. In fact, not a word to anyone. I'm trusting you, man to man."

"What about Geoff?"

"Oh, Geoff's not interested. He likes making things and doing things, he doesn't care about the money side. No, this is specially for you, Barry. *You're* the one who's in my confidence about this."

Father spoke as if conferring a great privilege. I waited.

"Borrowed," he said. He paused for effect. "Borrowed, every penny of it."

I was puzzled.

"I thought you didn't believe in borrowing," I said. "How are you going to pay it all back?"

"In normal times," Father said, "I wouldn't believe in borrowing. You're quite right. But these times are not normal. And to survive, Barry, you know what you have to do? You have to adapt. Ever heard of evolution?"

"As a matter of fact, yes," I said.

"Then you should know about adapting. That's why we don't still live in trees. We adapted so as to live in houses. When times change, a wise man changes his ideas. Now listen, Barry, this year I've borrowed about half a million."

I whistled.

"Installment credit, bank loans, finance houses, anywhere I could get it. The papers are all in my new desk over there. I could tell you the exact amount at five minutes' notice. But in round figures that's the sum. Half a million pounds. And you know what all that borrowing will be, by the end of this winter?"

The word came to my mind.

"Paper," I said.

"Yes. If I'm right, it will just be paper. Waste paper." Father smiled again. "And here am I with a good house—a gentleman's house, you could almost say—and enough of everything already to see us through for quite a while. A pity I couldn't raise sufficient to fit the place out as I'd like, but food stocks come first, and I haven't finished building them up yet. As for the debts, they don't worry me, because as I say they'll soon be waste paper."

Geoff had come into the room while Father was speaking.

"What's that about waste paper?" he inquired.

"A figure of speech, lad," said Father. "Worthless money, that's what it means."

"Oh," said Geoff without much interest.

Father turned to me again.

"We'll come out of this all right, Barry, you mark my words. Intelligence, adaptability, forethought, that's what you need to have. And those who haven't got it will pay the price."

Suddenly distaste rose in me; I felt for myself what had upset Stuart Hazell on the day of our conversation in the shop, what had nauseated Nessie as we stood in the cellar surveying the loaded racks. I looked at Geoff, wondering how he'd react to the statement that people who weren't clever enough to look after themselves would have to suffer. But there was no response in his eyes; he wasn't really listening.

"Now, remember what I said, Barry," Father went on. "Discretion, that's what's needed. Keep your knowledge to yourself. Above all, don't trust the womenfolk. Women always talk. And, Barry . . ."

"Yes?"

"I was impressed the other day by that remark that if people can't buy or borrow, they'll beg or steal. True enough. But if folk learned what we have here, then when the hard times come we might be up against something worse than begging or even stealing."

Geoff, who'd sat down with a football paper, looked up now.

"What do you mean by that, Dad?" he inquired.

"Well, I won't spell it out. Not just now, anyway. But to my way of thinking, it's a rule of life that when you've got what you want, the next problem is to hold onto what you've got. What we've worked so hard to collect, we may have to defend."

"You mean, somebody might try to take if off us? By force?"

"It's not impossible."

"Don't worry, Dad," said Geoff. "I reckon we could keep an army at bay here."

Father smiled proudly and put an arm round Geoff's shoulders. "There speaks my lad," he said.

5

LATE JANUARY. Still no snow. Fine, clear, crisp days when the sky stayed icy blue and the morning frost was hard as diamond. Lovely weather, if you had food, a warm house, thick clothes. But there were more and more people this January who hadn't.

We heard about it in talk after talk after talk, on television or in current affairs classes at school. The difference between the way things were now and the kind of crisis talk we'd been hearing for years was that now you could go outside and see for yourself what was happening.

The cost of living had doubled in a month. People who were in work were still not doing too badly. They got their wages increased each week and spent them the day they came, before everything went up again. But there were so many who weren't in work. Father's shop, cutting its staff by more than half, was only a tiny example. The plastics factory on the new industrial estate behind our school had closed altogether, because it couldn't get the foreign currency it needed to buy its raw materials. Industries all over the country were in the same position. It was just as Father had said. Nobody wanted our currency anymore. Swiss francs, yes; gold, yes; paper, no. Money was dying.

The lines at the employment exchange lengthened. There were beginning to be queues at the shops, too. Rationing had been brought in suddenly, at a day's notice, after repeated warnings that it might have to come but denials that it was actually imminent. Now we had little squares of thin smudgily printed paper that entitled each of us to buy four ounces of meat a week, two ounces of bacon and butter and cheese, and a daily half pound of bread. But you had to find these things first, to say nothing of finding the money to pay for them. Supermarkets sold out by midmorning, and it was said that far more people would have been turned away if there weren't so many who couldn't afford to take up their rations.

In some ways it was beginning to feel like living in a bad film. You couldn't believe in what was happening, but it was true; or perhaps nothing was true anymore. You just had to let life wash over you. Many things went on as usual, but with a grotesque feeling of unreality about them. We still went to school and had the same lessons. "These are stirring times," our English teacher told us. "All we need is something in the pot to stir." Even the groans were halfhearted.

The school midday dinner—getting dearer week by week—now consisted mainly of vegetables, which still weren't rationed. Usually there was gravy, and occasionally a scrap of meat. But although the food wasn't appetizing, the plates were scraped clean. The principal's complaints about waste, which had gone on for years, ceased almost overnight. There was no waste now. And overcrowding in the dining hall ceased as well, because there were so many children whose parents couldn't pay for the meal anymore. These were usually the least well nourished.

At Rose Grove we ate well but frugally. Father was still managing to accumulate stores, but only very slowly, and not with his old urgency. He was inclined to go to the smaller shops, for reasons which I didn't understand until the day in the school holidays when he couldn't get away from work and sent me to Mr. Turp's corner butchery for the meat rations.

When I got to the shop, Mr. Turp was just turning an elderly would-be customer away. "See for yourself," he was saying, waving an arm around in the direction of his empty slabs. "Not enough to feed a bluebottle."

I turned to follow the customer out, but Mr. Turp called me back. He was a small sharp man with spectacles—not at all the kind of person you'd think of as a butcher.

"You're Norman Mortimer's boy, aren't you?" he asked.

I nodded.

"I think I might find something for you. Where's your tickets?"

I handed them over. Mr. Turp went behind the scenes and reappeared with a small wrapped package.

"Lamb chops," he said. "They're quite nice. Can't give you any choice, I'm afraid. You're lucky to get anything. You've just seen that for yourself."

"Yes," I said. "I don't quite understand why . . ."

"Don't trouble your head about it, lad. That'll be just two hundred pounds. Official controlled price."

I handed the money over: a few crumpled notes.

"Time was when that would have been a lot," Mr. Turp said. "Now it's like the pretend money you use in a game. I don't know why I bother to take it." He did take it, all the same. "Put the meat in your bag, quickly," he said. "And don't go just yet. There's old Mr. Briggs again. Wait till I've finished with him."

The elderly customer had come back into the shop. This time his equally elderly wife was with him.

"We were wondering, Mr. Turp," he said. "We were wondering if you might happen to have some bones around. Just a few bones that we could buy."

"Bones, Mr. Briggs? There's no bones in this shop. Only my own old bones. And yours, of course." Mr. Turp laughed heartily. Then he said, with an air of generosity, "Wait a minute. I might just have something back there. I'll have a really good look around for you."

He came back with a package of bones wrapped up in newspaper, which he opened to show the old couple. A little meat still clung to the bones. They eyed it eagerly.

"How much, Mr. Turp?" the old man asked.

"Nothing, Mr. Briggs, nothing. Take it with my compliments."

"Thank you, Mr. Turp. I'm—we're—very grateful."

"Don't mention it, Mr. Briggs."

The old pair shuffled out. Mr. Turp turned to me again.

"Actually," he said, "I'm afraid I told that old chap a little white lie when he first came in. I do have a certain amount of stuff. But there's no point in selling it at controlled price to old age pensioners. Might almost as well give it away."

"You sold at controlled price to *me*."

"Yes, lad, yes." Mr. Turp leaned over the counter thoughtfully. "You're not quite the same. You're Norman Mortimer's lad. Your name's Barry, isn't it? Well, Barry, as I was saying, I do have a certain amount of stuff around. And I don't sell it on the black market, I may add. Oh, I know there are some who do. Ten times the proper price they ask, and get it, too. I wouldn't do that. Besides—" and his voice dropped suddenly from a virtuous to a knowing note—"it's still only paper money, isn't it? Now, Barry, your dad runs a shoe shop. My wife and me, we could both do with a new pair of winter shoes. I reckon me and your dad could do a deal. His shoes, my meat. Fair exchange is no robbery, eh?"

I didn't say anything.

"Just mention it to your dad, will you, Barry? Don't worry, there's nothing illegal about it. Nothing at all. But I'd rather you didn't say anything to anyone *except* your dad, all the same. You don't want to go putting thoughts into people's heads, do you? Just tell him, quietly, from me. Meat for shoes, shoes for meat. Fair exchange no robbery."

I made noncommittal noises and got out of the shop as soon as I could. I didn't say anything to Father. But Mr. Turp must have made contact with him somehow. A few evenings later I saw that Father had brought a familiar-shaped parcel home from work. Obviously some shoes were still available. When Father went out after dinner, he took the parcel with him. Next morning our refrigerator was full of fresh meat. The deep freeze in the basement was crammed with it already.

"Barry, did you hear that?" Nessie asked me urgently at breakfast.

"Hear what?"

"On the radio."

"I wasn't listening."

"Oh, for crying out loud. Look, we might be in time to get it on the other channel if we switch over. Come in the other room."

We took the radio to the big bleak sitting room. I stood cold and impatient while Nessie fiddled with it.

"Never mind that, just *tell* me!" I begged her. But Nessie gestured at me to be quiet. And a minute later she did indeed pick up what she wanted on a different news bulletin.

There were to be strong measures against hoarders and black marketeers. Hoarders would be sent to prison, the government was saying, as well as fined. And their hoards would be confiscated. Prosecutions for black market deals would be stepped up. And it was illegal to barter rationed goods. That would lead to prison, too.

Nessie and I looked at each other in dismay as the list of threats and warnings was reeled out in a sharp, incisive newscaster voice that made you feel there might be a rap at the door any moment. The bulletin finished with the offer of a way out to people who might be running into bigger trouble than they'd thought. Hoarders who turned their stocks in within the next week wouldn't be prosecuted or asked any questions. But after that they'd get no mercy.

"Well . . ." I said as the bulletin ended.

"We'd better tell him, hadn't we?"

"No need. He'll hear it. He keeps up with the news."

"Is it any good suggesting?" Nessie asked.

"Suggesting that he should turn his stuff in? Now, honestly, Nessie, what do *you* think? Would he be likely to?"

"No, of course he wouldn't. Not a chance. But oh, Barry, if only . . . You know, I'd much rather we were in Terry's position. They don't know where their next meal's coming from, but they survive, they're in it like everyone else. If it has to be potatoes again, well, it's potatoes again."

"How long will there be potatoes?" I asked.

I had guiltily mixed feelings. When I thought of the old couple eyeing those bones with scraps of meat clinging to them, I felt sickened and ashamed. Yet at the same time I had a sneaking sense of comfort from remembering our own well-stocked basement.

"Should we just *try* telling him it might be safer to turn everything in?" Nessie said. But her tone of voice was less than halfhearted. She knew well enough what the response to such a suggestion would be.

"No point," I said. "No point at all. It'd only make him distrust us. We'll have more influence if he thinks we're on his side."

"I suppose so," Nessie admitted reluctantly.

"And you know something else, Nessie? We're stuck with it now. It's *no good* having misgivings. You might as well squash them. He's absolutely determined, and now he's outside the law. And we're helpless. You wouldn't do anything that might send him to prison, would you?"

Nessie swallowed and shook her head.

"No," she said. "No, damn him. Damn and blast him, no. But has it struck you, Barry? From now on, we're going to have to watch it every minute of every day in case somebody lets the cat out of the bag and *does* send him to prison. It doesn't have to be intentional. It could easily happen by accident. And anybody might do it. Even us."

6

THE BEGINNING OF FEBRUARY. Still cold, and not so fine. It was a harsh gray Saturday morning, the kind of day when people say it's too cold for snow. There were in fact a few tiny specks of snow floating in the air but not adding up to anything. Nessie was standing at the sitting room window, waiting for Terry to appear in the drive, and telling me in the meantime of her worries about Ellen.

Since the departure of her dog Peggy, Ellen had been withdrawn and sulky. It wasn't too difficult for her to slip away to Terry's house and see Peggy; but after the first week or two she hardly ever went—not because she had stopped caring about Peggy, but because each visit left her feeling upset and tearful. Peggy welcomed her but was obviously quite happy with the Timpsons. Ellen returned to a more childish phase of her life and carried her old teddy bear around the house with her. Father's discouragement of visiting children had left her without friends. Sometimes she sat watching television, with the bear hugged to her chest. Sometimes she and the bear were engaged in long mysterious conversations, which ceased if anyone came near. Sometimes she just sat, and it was impossible to tell what she was thinking.

Strangely, it was through Ellen that the first small leak of information occurred. A few days before the present Saturday, she'd been asked to a birthday party by a child in her class. Nessie was anxious that she should go; and as the party wasn't being held on our premises Father had no objection. Ellen herself showed little enthusiasm, maintaining that nobody liked her and that Janet had only asked her because the whole class was invited. Several times Ellen insisted that she wasn't going; but when the actual day came she slipped off to the party without telling any of us, and afterward she admitted grudgingly that she'd had quite a good time.

This Saturday morning Father was at work; for, little as there now was to sell, the shop still stayed open on Saturdays. After a few minutes of waiting for Terry, Nessie called me over to the window. Coming up the drive was a small, hesitant group of children. They nudged one another as they approached, and urged one another on. None of them, it seemed, had quite the courage to go up to the front door.

"They look like Ellen's age group," Nessie said. "That's nice. She does need some children to play with. I'll go and let them in."

But the doorbell rang before she got there, and it was Geoff, crossing the hall, who answered the door. So he and Nessie and I were all there to greet the children; only Ellen herself, last seen talking to her teddy bear in the rear quarters of the house, was missing.

There were half a dozen children in the group. One was older than the rest and a little taller: a thin girl in her teens whom I'd seen around at school but whose name I couldn't remember. She hung behind the rest of the group as if she didn't really belong. The one who was pushed forward to act as spokesman was Billy Willett, aged about twelve. And he was extremely shy and embarrassed.

"It's about the ham," he said.

"Ham?"

"The ham that Ellen brought to our Janet's party."

All three of us looked at one another, alarmed. Geoff went back down the hall and shouted, "Ellen! El-l-en!"

"I don't really know what you're talking about," Nessie said casually.

"The ham. Ellen brought it. She brought it to the party. It was lovely, wasn't it, Janet?"

"Yes, it was lovely," Janet said. She licked her lips involuntarily.

"Our mum had a bit, too," Billy said. "She told us she'd nearly forgotten what ham was like, it's so long since we had any."

Geoff had returned with a fidgety Ellen in tow, still clutching her teddy bear.

"What are you getting at, Billy?" he demanded bluntly.

Billy was still embarrassed.

"Well," he said, "Ellen told us there was more at home. So I wondered if we could have some as a surprise for my mum, because she liked it so much. My gran likes ham, too."

"It's my mum's birthday soon, as well," Janet explained anxiously. "Her birthday's only a week after mine. When I was on the way, she thought I might have the same birthday as her, but I was . . ."

"Ssshh, Janet!" Billy said. "It isn't that. But truly, our mum was saying the other day she was at her wits' end, and we thought, well, if they really have plenty at Ellen's

86

house, p'raps we could borrow some till things get better. Of course, Mum doesn't know we've come."

Nessie and I stared at Ellen, who went red and then white.

"Did you take a can of ham to Janet's party?" Nessie asked.

"Well, I . . ."

"Two cans," said Billy.

It was Geoff who dealt with the situation, and dealt with it ruthlessly.

"It was a couple of leftover cans," he said. "Just something we found in a corner of the cellar, and my mum thought they'd help out with the party. We haven't any more. No more at all."

There was a little disappointed chorus of "Ohs." The older girl at the back turned away. I realized that she was in tears. The others still hung about the door as if they couldn't quite accept Geoff's statement.

"I'm sorry," Geoff said, patiently but firmly, "but that's the way it is." And he closed the door on them.

"Well, let's hope that satisfies them," he said.

"Did you have to do that, Geoff?" Nessie asked.

"Yes, he did," I said. "What else could he do? Give the whole game away?"

"Oh, my God!" Nessie said. "Yes. Yes, you're right. But how obnoxious. Why does Dad have to be like he is? Why?"

"You ought to be glad he's like he is," Geoff said. "So stop knocking him, can't you?"

"Why can't we just be in the same boat as everybody else? Oh, I hate concealment. I hate, hate, hate it!"

"That's all right for *you*, Nessie," Geoff said. And then,

"Isn't anybody going to ask this wretched kid what she's been up to?"

Ellen, shaken by the episode, looked appealingly to Nessie for defense. But Nessie was shaken, too, in a different way.

"What happened, Ellen?" I asked. "Where did you get those cans of ham?"

"I got them from the basement," Ellen said in a very small voice.

"Who said you could?"

"Nobody said I could."

"How did you know they were there?"

Ellen, still frightened, said nothing.

"How did you know?" Geoff repeated.

"Can't you leave the child alone?" Nessie demanded.

Ellen clutched Nessie's hand. I could see a row coming up.

"There, Ellen," I said mildly. "Just tell us what happened."

"I thought I'd like to take something nice for the party," Ellen said.

"What made you think there were things in the basement?"

"Oh, I knew."

"You'd been down there?"

"Oh, yes."

"But why? How? It's always kept locked."

"I often saw Daddy going up and down. I knew where there was a key."

"And didn't you know you had no business to be down there, taking things without permission?" I said.

"Hell's teeth!" said Nessie. "Are you going to tell her

it's wrong to take from a hoarder and give to people who are without?"

"I don't know what to tell her," I said.

"Oh, don't fuss!" said Geoff. "Listen, Ellen. First, you leave all that stuff down there alone. Second, if the kids ask you any more about it, you say you were only pretending you could get more, so as to make yourself important. And third, not a word to a soul about our basement. Right?"

"Yes, Geoff," said Ellen meekly.

"Now show me where you took the cans from. We'll try and cover up so Dad won't ever know. And if ever I find you've done this again I'll bash you. Understand?"

"Yes, Geoff."

"Who do you think you are, Geoff?" Nessie asked. Her manner was getting wild; I thought she was on the brink of hysteria.

"I think I'm the only one who knows what to do," Geoff said. "While you two are tripping over your consciences, I get on with it."

"My father, right or wrong," Nessie said sardonically.

"That'll do for me," Geoff said.

"Then heaven help you."

"Heaven help us all if it wasn't for Dad."

The doorbell rang loudly in my ear. I opened the door automatically. It was Terry. I'd forgotten he was due to arrive any minute.

"Hello," he said, seeing all four of us gathered in the hallway, just inside the front door. "Family reunion, eh?" He looked down at Ellen's tear-stained face. "Hello, treasure. What's the matter? Tell your old friend Terry what the matter is."

89

Ellen pursed her lips resolutely together and said nothing.

"Still upset about your Peggy, eh?" said Terry sympathetically. "Peggy's all right. Though of course she's missing you. Me and Mum's not the same, are we? Guess she knows we're not her real owners." He tickled Ellen under the chin. "Here, why don't you come with us and see her? We could all take her a walk. You don't mind, Nessie, do you? We'll go with Ellen and take Peggy a walk, eh? You and me can be together some other time."

"All right," Nessie said, abstractedly.

"Not all right," said Geoff. "There's something Ellen and I have to see to, isn't there, Ellen?"

But at this Ellen burst into fresh tears. Terry surveyed her with half-real, half-comic dismay.

"Watery day today," he remarked. And then, to us all, "Hey, did you know there's a kid sitting on the wall opposite your front gate, sobbing her heart out? *She* wouldn't say what it was about, either. Nobody confides in Terry these days."

"Who was it?" I asked. "Did you know her?" The older girl who'd wept when Geoff turned the children away was still haunting my mind.

"Dark-haired kid with big eyes," Terry said. "Seen her before, but I don't know her." Then, to Ellen, "Pity I didn't bring any blotting paper. Dry up, treasure. Sure you're not coming?"

"Go on, Ellen," said Geoff, relenting. "We'll have time later to do what we have to do."

Ellen stopped crying. She dried her eyes with some dignity. Then she said, in a formal, polite little voice, "No, thank you, Terry, I'm not coming." She seemed suddenly a year or two older. She and Geoff disappeared, hand in hand, toward the back of the house. Terry looked after them and shrugged his shoulders comically.

"Something funny going on," he remarked. "This house is the place for funny things, isn't it?"

"And for not-so-funny ones," said Nessie.

"I suppose I'd better not ask what it's all about?"

"No, I think you'd better not."

"In our house, anybody can join in and anybody does."

"This isn't your house," Nessie said. "Or anything like it." She sighed. Terry kissed her lightly on the forehead and put an arm round her.

"Come on," he said. "Out of it. Looks like the U.S. Marines came to the rescue just in time."

I watched them walk, arms round each other, down the drive. Mother had been ironing in the kitchen while this morning's events went on, and I supposed she was still ironing. I felt very much alone.

Five minutes later the thought of the girl with the big dark eyes was still lingering in my mind. On a day like this, she could hardly still be around. But I needed to stretch my legs, didn't I? On impulse I put my thick coat on and made my way down the drive. There was no crunch in the unyielding gravel; the dark gloomy rhododendron leaves were frozen into a rigid droop. Too cold for snow indeed. A bitter day, when your cheeks were icily pinched and you knew your gloved fingers and shod toes would freeze before you'd gone far.

She wasn't in the drive or on the wall opposite. How could she have been, on a day like this? She'd gone. Of course she'd gone. And why should I care? She was at my school, I'd seen her around, I could see her any time. There was nothing special about today. There was nothing special about *her*. But I did care.

A raincoated figure was just disappearing round the next corner. Could that be her? She hadn't been wearing a raincoat like that, had she? I wasn't sure.

I ran after the person I'd seen, and followed into the next street, breath steaming in the cold air, shoes clattering on the metaled road. Hearing my approach, the figure turned. And it wasn't her. It was a small, thin, tight-faced housewife, fifty years old if a day. How could I have thought . . .?

The woman walker looked apprehensive as I ran toward her. There'd been a number of attacks lately on unescorted women, even in daylight. Nowadays they rarely carried shopping bags in quiet streets, for fear of inviting assault. And wise people didn't send young children to the shops. But once I'd clattered past her, the woman was no more interested in me than I in her.

And there, thirty yards ahead of her, was the girl. I kept on running, drew up alongside her, and fell into step. The girl was smaller than I was, and she looked up at me, wondering. She wasn't crying now.

I realized I had no idea what to say to her. I felt my cheeks redden, which wasn't usual with me. And then, looking at her, I could see there was deep trouble in her face.

"I'm Barry Mortimer," I said.

"Yes, I know."

"I saw you at our house just now."

"Yes."

"I'm . . . sorry there wasn't anything."

"You don't have to be sorry. Nobody had any right anyway. It was cheek. I suppose you expect it in little kids. But I'm bigger. Older, anyway. So I'm the one who ought to be sorry."

I hadn't anything to say to that.

"A few weeks ago even, I'd have been ashamed," the girl said. "Now I'm not ashamed. It doesn't matter. Things like that don't matter. It's a luxury, being ashamed. I'd rather be ashamed than hungry, any day."

"You're hungry?"

"No. Not really. I'm not talking about *me* being hungry, if you know what I mean. I'm all right."

"You're thin."

"I always was thin."

"Anyway, if you don't mean *you* being hungry, what *do* you mean?"

"Oh, I . . . Look, it isn't anything to do with you, truly it isn't. I'm not telling you to mind your own business. I just mean there isn't anything you can do. I'm sorry I came with those kids. I shouldn't have done."

"Why were you with them, anyway?"

"Oh, I used to take Janet to school when she was smaller, and I go there sometimes, and I was just helping out with her party. It was quite a good party, really, though if it hadn't been for Ellen there'd have been nothing but a bit of bread-and-spread to eat. Poor souls, they've not much more than we have."

We had been walking downhill from the Mount toward the city.

"Listen," I said. "You talk about being hungry, but you say it isn't you. And you talk about 'we.' Who's hungry? Who's 'we'?"

She hung back and turned her face from me toward

the hedge of the house we were passing. I realized that she was trying not to cry again, and felt embarrassed. But after half a minute she was all right.

"My mother," she said. "She's been ill. Now you know. And there's nothing you can do, Barry. I'm sorry you had to bother. So go home and forget it."

I didn't want to go home and I didn't think I could forget it.

"Where do you live?" I asked her.

"Just a bit lower down. Not far."

"And what's your name?"

"Wendy. Wendy Farrar."

"Hello, Wendy." I smiled at her.

"Hello." She smiled, wanly.

"Take me to see your mum."

"Why, Barry? Why should you want to see her? It wouldn't do any good."

"Why not? I can meet a person's mum if I want, can't I?"

"I'm not sure. I have to think about her before anyone else."

"You said she's ill?"

"Not exactly. She's *been* ill. She's kind of recovering. I don't know whether you ought to see her. . . . Look, Barry, we live just round the next corner. You can come in if you want while I have a word with her."

The street was one of small semidetached houses, all alike and characterless, each with its small enclosed garden. Each had a bay window and a small wooden porch like a sentry box. Even the garden gates—wrought iron with a rising sun pattern—were identical.

Wendy's was number 44. Only knowing the number

would have enabled anybody to tell it from any other in the street.

We went in through the back door. And inside it was still cold. Our breath was visible in the chilly air.

We were in a kitchen, clean but not well equipped, with a plain deal table, an old-fashioned sink, plenty of cupboards, but no modern units.

"My dad died three years ago," Wendy said. "Mum's never worked. She's not strong. She has a pension, of course. But . . ."

She didn't need to finish that sentence. Pensions fixed in money terms weren't worth anything anymore. An amount that would have been a decent annual income five years ago might just about buy you a week's food now, if you were careful and if you could find it. By next month, quite probably it wouldn't buy a loaf of bread.

There were state pensions as well. But they'd never been generous. And although they were now being increased month by month, the increases were never enough to make up for the continuing fall in the value of money. You might still just manage to feed yourself on the state pension, provided you could find a shop that had the food and would sell it at the controlled price. But you had to be prepared to hunt around and to queue. You hadn't to be discouraged if you waited in line for an hour and then found that stocks had run out just before it was your turn. For a person in poor health it was a grim outlook.

"You might as well see for yourself," Wendy said. She opened the door to a pantry. And the contrast with our basement was pathetic. A few small jars and bottles held (I supposed) powders and pastes and spices and sauces.

Nothing nourishing in those. Almost every other shelf was empty. The butt end of a loaf of bread lay face down on a breadboard. In a basket were a few potatoes. Wendy opened the door of a meat safe. It was empty. She opened the refrigerator. That was empty, too.

"There you are," she said. "That's how things are."

"Are you going to starve?" I asked, appalled.

"Oh, no," she said. "We've been promised bread later today. And Mr. Birkett said he'd have more vegetables tomorrow. And Mr. Turp keeps saying he'll have some meat for our tickets soon, and I suppose he will sometime. I wish I was prettier."

"You *what?*"

"I wish I was prettier. That makes a difference at the shops. They find you something if they like the look of you. In fact, they say some of them . . ."

"Some of them what?"

"Oh, nothing!"

"Wendy!" A voice floated faintly down the stairs.

"That's Mum," Wendy said. She didn't seem sorry to be interrupted. "Coming! Wait here a minute, Barry."

The minute was a fairly long one. I stamped my feet and blew on my frozen fingers. When Wendy reappeared, she said, "You can come up if you like, Barry. Mum'd like to see you, and she's fairly well this morning. But you don't have to, you know. She'd understand. It's—well, I suppose it's a sickroom."

It was a clean, bare room. Like the rest of the house, it suggested a long-standing shortage of money rather than a sudden disaster. The woman sitting up in bed had long dark hair flowing over a dressing gown which she held closely round herself, so that I couldn't see anything of her but face and hair. A very small electric fire beamed

96

a little frail warmth toward her; a book lay face down on the coverlet.

Her face was pale and thin, her eyes big like Wendy's, but her voice sounded surprisingly normal, and her tone was friendly and sensible.

"Hello," she said. "Sorry to receive you like this. It's silly, isn't it? I've had flu. One of the bugs that are around just now. It's the time of year. Don't worry, I'm not infectious. Just feeble. I'm all right while I stay here, but as soon as I start to move around I flop."

"I'll make you a hot drink," Wendy said. "We've got some meat cubes."

"Perhaps Barry would like one, too."

"No, no," I said hastily. "No, thank you."

"Are you sure?"

"Quite sure. I don't really like that sort of thing, truly I don't."

"Don't sound so anxious, Barry." Mrs. Farrar smiled. "It's funny in a kind of way. I'd never have thought the day would come when people would worry over a meat cube."

"It doesn't seem funny to *me*," said Wendy sternly. "And I worry about *you*."

Mrs. Farrar raised her eyebrows and smiled quizzically at me as Wendy went down to the kitchen.

"You wouldn't think it to look at her," she said, "but Wendy is bossy. And getting more so. I suppose it's to be expected. I can't do much, even when I'm not ill, and I certainly seem to get anything that's going. She's the mainstay. It's very frustrating, Barry, I can tell you, even in normal times. And in times like these it would make all the difference if I had a job."

She smiled at me again. She didn't sound sorry for

97

herself. But I was shaken by the contrast between this house and Terry's. The Timpsons weren't well-to-do, but they were always warm and never quite without food. Of course, Terry was in work, and his mother was healthy and could go round the shops and stand in line. And whatever else was short, they always had firewood and potatoes. I knew how they got firewood. I didn't know where the potatoes came from, but one of these days no doubt they'd tell me; Terry's wasn't a house of secrets. The Farrars were much worse off, with Wendy's mother in bed and Wendy at school all week.

A thought struck me then.

"Does Wendy have school dinners?" I asked.

"No. We can't afford them. A week's dinners would cost more than my pension. She takes a sandwich, if we have bread."

Mrs. Farrar's voice sounded weary now. And when Wendy came back with a hot drink in a mug, she saw signs in her mother's face that I hadn't noticed, and said sternly, "You're tired."

"I'm not tired, I'm better. I'll be up and around before long."

"You *are* tired. Lie back against that pillow."

Wendy adjusted the pillow and lifted her mother so that she was supported by it. Seeing her do so, I realized how light Mrs. Farrar must be. She was still clutching the dressing gown round her. I suspected that this was to conceal a painful thinness.

"I'm taking Barry away now," Wendy said.

Mrs. Farrar smiled and didn't object. "It was nice to meet you, Barry," she said.

Downstairs, I said to Wendy, "There must be something that somebody can do. Have you tried everything?" Actually, I'd only the vaguest idea what services were available. "Social Security? Home helps? Meals-on-wheels?"

"Barry," she said, "those services are so overstrained they can't do a thing. Maybe you don't realize, but I do, because I have to. There are hundreds of thousands of people in trouble, millions maybe. Of course, they're all in trouble separately, at home, so you don't *see* them. But there're just too many. As for my mother, it's not a case of 'Somebody ought to do something.' Those days are past. There isn't any 'somebody' anymore. There's only us."

"And what about *me*? Can't I help?"

"I don't know what you could do. Thank you all the same." She was beginning to sound a little remote, as if her mind was on something else. "I'm going to the baker's now. There's supposed to be bread at twelve."

"It's not quite eleven," I said.

"Heavens, I didn't know it was so late. I must rush. That's none too soon. If you're not well up in the queue you don't stand a chance."

"I'll come and wait in line with you," I offered.

"No, don't do that, Barry. It's only wasting your time. And truly, it doesn't help. I told you, a girl on her own often does better. Thank you all the same."

It was the second time she'd thanked me "all the same." I felt myself dismissed.

"All right," I said. "The baker's is down the hill and I go up the hill, so I suppose we'll be going different ways. Can I see you again?"

"Come when you like. If I'm in, I'm in. It would be nice to see you, of course it would."

"Good-bye, then."

I walked thoughtfully back up the Mount. Two things bothered me. One was the huge hopeless number of people needing help that the social services couldn't give. Surely it was still true that "Somebody ought to do something," and that somebody included myself. I hadn't talked for a long time to Cliff, who was involved in the meals-on-wheels service, or to Stuart Hazell, who was a moving spirit in Share Alike. They were doing something, I wasn't. It was time I got in touch with them.

The other thought that troubled me was that it still wouldn't be any use relying on some all-powerful "them" to help Mrs. Farrar as an individual. If anything was to be done, I'd have to do it myself. And of course there was something I could do.

Ellen had shown the way. But it was a way that frightened me to death.

7

FOR OUR MAIN MEAL that evening we had soup, roast shoulder of lamb, baked potatoes, peas and carrots, and a jam sponge pudding. It gave Mother pleasure to cook and serve a meal like that. I thought Father might complain that it was too lavish. But he said not a word. Mother, from much experience, had chosen her occasion well. Father was in an extremely good mood. He'd done some kind of a deal that afternoon—I didn't know exactly what—which had added substantially to his stores. The car had stood for some time at the top of the area steps, and Father and Geoff had been busy unloading and stacking.

I didn't enjoy the meal much. Nor, I thought, did Nessie. Several times our eyes met guiltily across the table. Ellen was only picking at her food. But Father and Geoff ate heartily, with the air of people who'd earned it. And in spite of my lack of pleasure in it, I ate well myself. Just as I had, horribly, had to admit to a feeling of comfort at seeing all our stocks, so the thought of lines of people queuing in the cold for bread or vegetables caused me to feel a curious, self-disgusting satisfaction in filling my own belly.

It served me right that I slept poorly and had bad dreams. They were mostly about Wendy and her mother. And my dreams kept confusing and distorting them, so that I saw a skeletally thin Mrs. Farrar standing behind and dwarfing the group of children at our front door, and I saw a dressing-gown-huddled Wendy propped against pillows in a room as vast as a cathedral.

At five in the morning I was awake. It was still dark. And although in daylight I might have thought better of it, in the darkness before dawn I had no doubt about what I must do. I put on a dressing gown and pulled out from the bottom of a wardrobe the rucksack I'd taken to school camp the previous summer. I crept down to the laundry room—quietly, but not in any state of fright, for the excursion had something of the unreality of dream still clinging to it. I felt behind the washing machine. The key to the basement was not there.

I think if I'd been fully awake I would have concluded that Father had removed the key for security reasons, and I'd have abandoned my idea with a certain amount of relief and gone back to bed. As it was, I felt myself under a compulsion that wouldn't let me give up so easily. I found a flashlight in the kitchen and went down the concrete cellar steps in the forlorn hope that the door at the bottom might have been left open. It was an absurd hope, because Father was the last man to forget to lock a door.

Yet open it was. And along the edge of the partition that separated the first, innocent-seeming cellar, with its tools and garden equipment, from the main basement, I could see a sliver of feeble light. From somewhere beyond came the shuffling and scraping sounds of human movement: not loud, but clearly audible in the night silence. Then there was a series of metallic clicks.

My first thought was of an intruder. It didn't immediately strike my sleep-stupid mind that a burglar wouldn't have been likely to find the key and open the cellar door with it. Nor did it strike me that my obvious move was to creep quietly back up the steps and rouse Father. Instead I tiptoed through the first cellar, edged my way round the partition, and moved quietly between the racks toward the source of the sound. The small dim light at the far end of the basement was on, and the loaded racks threw oddly shaped shadows, angular or bumpy. There was something sinister and menacing about the sight, but I still had a sense of unreality that prevented me from being as frightened as I might otherwise have been.

Then I saw who was there. It was Father himself. He was sitting at his little battered desk in the corner, beneath that feeble light, with his back to me. He was fully dressed. It looked from the back-and forth movement of his elbow as if he was engaged in some task of a brushing or rubbing kind.

The sight of Father woke me up. Why should he be down here at such an hour? He could go into the basement at any time; he didn't have to conceal himself, and he never in fact bothered to do so. He was the head of the house and he went where he liked; that was his attitude. Seeing him now, I felt physically apprehensive. I had always been a little afraid of him. But for the moment compulsion still drove me. I moved a few feet toward him, slipping across the open space between one sheltering rack and the next. Father's movements stopped, and

I heard a sharp hiss of breath. But he hadn't become aware of me; I had the impression that he'd hurt himself in some minor way—a finger caught in something, perhaps. Another man might have sworn to himself, but Father never swore.

Then, suddenly and without conscious thought, I knew that my stealthy approach was the wrong one. As silently as I'd come, I made my way back to the top of the cellar steps. I switched the light on, came boldly down the steps, and marched through to the main basement, shouting, "Who's there?"

Father was taken by surprise. He got up, turned round, and took a step or two toward me, keeping between me and the desk. There was a piece of rag in his hand.

"You!" I said. "Whatever are you doing down here at this hour?"

As always when he was unexpectedly confronted, I could feel the tension in Father. After a momentary pause he stepped aside so that I could see what was on the desk. Something small, metallic, lethal.

"A revolver!" I exclaimed.

"That's right. A service revolver."

"Wherever did you get it?"

"I've had it a long time. Since the last war. Official issue. I was an officer, you know."

"I didn't know they let people keep things like that."

"They don't. But it's been known to happen."

"It seems in pretty good condition."

"It's in excellent condition. I look after things, Barry. I'm just wiping off the grease that I'd put it away in. Then it'll be ready for use."

"It would still fire?"

"It certainly would. If needed."

"And can you get ammunition for it?"

"It might be difficult now, but I've plenty. . . . Anyway, Barry, it's not your business to interrogate me. What are *you* doing down here?"

"I couldn't sleep. Thought I heard sounds down here, and it might have been burglars," I said. This wasn't untrue. And I added, going on the offensive again, "People in this country aren't allowed to carry guns. Oughtn't you to have handed it in?"

"I could have done, Barry. There've been several amnesties—times when you could hand in a gun without getting into trouble. But I chose not to. I always thought it would come in useful sometime."

"But it's dangerous. You could *kill* somebody with it."

"Quite right, Barry."

"And . . . well, we're not at war, are we?"

"Not quite. Not yet."

"You don't really mean things are going to be *that* bad? You wouldn't actually use a gun on people, whatever was happening, would you?"

"I don't know," my father said slowly. "I can imagine circumstances in which I would. But I hope it won't come to that. You don't *have* to kill folk with it. You might need to hold them off. Even the sight of a thing like this would scare the daylights out of most people. Or a shot fired in the air, just to demonstrate."

"It frightens *me*," I said, "just having it around."

"It isn't dangerous in the right hands, Barry. Mine are the right hands."

"Can you use it?"

"Of course I can use it. I was trained to use it. And other guns, too. I was a good shot, once."

"That was a long time ago."

"I don't think I'll have forgotten. All the same, I mean to get in some practice."

I was growing more rather than less uneasy.

"Listen," I said, "it's against the law, isn't it? You could be in trouble."

"Yes, it's against the law and I could be in trouble. So what? Storing the food I have here is illegal now, as well. Are you going to report me, Barry?"

I didn't say anything to that.

"You can if you like, you know. And it's the food that would bring the real trouble, not the gun. Why don't you report me, and let the family starve?"

He was pressing *me* now. I tried to seize the initiative again.

"You can't have wanted us to know you had a gun," I said slowly. "Or you wouldn't have come down here to clean it at five in the morning. There are plenty of other times."

"I didn't want to alarm anyone, Barry. I guessed that you or Nessie might overreact. Which is just what you have done. And anyway, I was awake early this morning. I thought I'd just get this small job done quietly. Before breakfast is a convenient time. Now, if you'll excuse me, I'll finish it."

He sat down at the desk and picked up the gun. Then he said, "I don't know how you managed to hear sounds coming from down here. This isn't a noisy job. You weren't . . . ?"

"Weren't what?"

I could almost see suspicion mounting in him.

"You weren't *spying* on me?"

"No, I was not. Absolutely not."

"I should hope not. Spies get no mercy, remember? I'm not sure that even a son of mine would get mercy for spying. . . . Here, what are you doing with that rucksack? What's inside it?"

"Nothing."

"Let me see."

"I told you, nothing."

"I said, 'Let me see.' "

"What's it to do with you? Why *should* there be anything in my rucksack? I tell you it's empty."

Then the obvious thought occurred to Father. He pounced.

"What was *going* to be in your rucksack?"

We stared at each other. I didn't need to reply. Before he'd finished asking the question, he knew the answer.

"You were going to steal from the racks," he said. And then, rapping out the words, *"Who for?"*

My knees were weak. This was a battle between us that had swayed to and fro, the initiative now mine, now his. But in a strange way I felt calm. I spoke very deliberately.

"I am taking something," I said, "to give to a girl whose mother is ill in bed."

Father's first reaction wasn't to the main point.

"You're too young to get involved with a girl," he said.

"I'm not involved. Nothing of that kind. They haven't enough to eat, that's all, and we have more than enough."

It seemed a long time before he said anything else. I could feel the fury in him intensifying, coming slowly to a cold boil.

"You stand there," he said, "and tell me you *are* taking something, just like that, without a by-your-leave. Who do you think you are, Barry Mortimer?"

"Your son," I said.

That silenced Father again for a while. Then he said, in a strained but reasonable tone, "Barry, I cannot feed all the lame ducks in the neighborhood. I cannot feed even one lame duck, because sooner or later the news would get around. Nor does it make much sense to feed just one out of so many. So now stop being ridiculous and go back to bed."

I was still calm. My calmness surprised myself. I'd never stood up to Father like this before.

"Father," I said. (I usually addressed him as Dad, but not this time.) "You're not in a position to tell me I can't do this. You said yourself, your stocks are illegal and you've no right to have that gun. You asked me if I'd report you. Well, if you stopped me now, I would. Excuse me."

I opened the rucksack. Then I turned my back on Father and walked without hurrying to a place in the racks where I remembered there were canned meats and fish.

With an appearance of leisurely selection, I took down cans of meatballs and chopped ham, of sardines and pilchards. My back was toward Father still. All the time I was putting the cans into the rucksack I felt a shrinking sensation of the flesh, a creeping apprehension that at any moment his arm might go round my neck, or his hands grip my shoulders, or his boot land in my backside. Or he might hit me with the gun. But none of these things happened.

The rucksack held more than I'd expected, and as the

cans went into it I began to feel a kind of guilt, an unexpected change in my feelings toward Father. This was his hoard, accumulated with enormous effort. Illegal it might be, but had I any right to help myself? With about a dozen cans in the sack, I found I couldn't bring myself to take any more. I turned to Father. He stood motionless, his face whitish yellow in the poor light, his hands rigid by his sides and telling me more eloquently than his voice could have done with what effort he restrained himself from using them on me.

"I've a few thousand pounds in the savings bank," I said. "Enough to pay for this lot, I should think. It's not the same as replacing them, but it's the best I can do."

"You needn't bother," Father said. His voice was barely audible. Then, "Are you proposing to make a habit of this, Barry?"

Asked the question five minutes earlier, I might have said, "Yes, I shall do it as often as I need." Now, in an odd way, I felt differently. And I had a sense of having gone as far as I could go, of having taken things precisely to the limit.

"I don't think I shall do it again," I said.

"I hope not," said my father. "There are six in the family, and you're only one of them. I don't think I could let anything stand in the way of my duty to the other five."

"Your duty?"

"My duty as I see it. I couldn't let anyone prevent me, Barry, even you. Now, take that bag and get out of here. Are you planning to tell anyone about tonight's events and what you've seen? Even your brother or your elder sister? Or this girl?"

"No," I said.

"I thought you wouldn't, Barry. I'm glad you won't. It saves me a painful decision. Good night, Barry—or should I say 'Good morning'?"

I didn't say either. I turned on my heel and went back to bed.

I put the cans in a neat pile on top of the Farrars' kitchen table. Wendy looked at me steadily over the top of them. She didn't ask me for any explanation, but I gave her one.

"They're a few we had in the basement," I said. "My father let me bring them."

"That was kind. I expect Mother will want to write and thank him."

"I think he'd rather she didn't."

"I see."

"Well . . . I suppose I should be going."

"Yes, Barry, I suppose so."

"Well . . . good-bye."

"Good-bye, Barry."

Oddly, I felt we were further apart. I had a sense of having explored a dead end, of failing to find a solution. Yet surely, I asked myself, surely her mother would be glad of the food?

"Yes, of course you can help us," Cliff said on the phone. "My goodness, we need it. Yes, your principal—what's his name? Jim Hibbert?—will give you the time off twice a week. At least, he has done for Stuart Hazell and two or three others. Come to the center on Wednesday at half past eleven. What brought you to this, Barry? There's too many people moving the other way, out of voluntary service. Can't blame them, I suppose. They've enough to do these days with looking after themselves."

"It's all very well if you *can* look after yourself," I said.

"Quite. I'm going to make a guess, Barry. I'm guessing that you've come across some actual person in trouble and seen what it's like."

"Yes, I have."

"I thought so. That tells you more than any amount of statistics. Now, you have a word with Mr. Hibbert, and all being well I'll see you on Wednesday."

"Well, Barry," I said to myself as I put the receiver down, "you've found a sop to your conscience."

8

STILL COLD, STILL GRAY. On the calendar the first week of February had gone by, but outside it felt as if January was lingering still. The old people in the queue outside the welfare center were capped and scarved and mufflered, many of them stamping their feet and hugging themselves and shivering.

I had known what street the center was in, but thought I might have trouble in finding the entrance. That, however, was one thing I didn't have to worry about. At a quarter past eleven the queue for the midday meal stretched right along the street and round the corner into the next.

"Those who are fit enough come here to the center for their dinner," Cliff explained, when I found him in a poky office at the back. "So many people need meals these days, we couldn't possibly take them all to their homes. Some arrive here at ten, to make sure of eating at twelve."

"It must be tough for them in the cold."

"Well, the really bitter weather cuts down the queue. It's too much for the older ones. Though plenty of them seem to be braving it today. Mike!"—this to one of his helpers. "The line's round the corner. Count out three hundred, will you? Then bring up the rear yourself. Any beyond three hundred you'll have to turn away. And watch out for people collapsing on the pavement; I'll be surprised if there aren't a few on a day like this. Stuart! Ask Pam to take over from me, will you? I'm going out on a round with you and Barry. High time I saw for myself how some of the customers are getting on."

With Cliff and Stuart Hazell I went out into the yard at the back. There was a line of medium-sized vans drawn up, all painted in inconspicuous neutral colors. Cliff backed one of them up to the kitchen entrance, and it was loaded with big oblong metal containers. Stuart carried several large vacuum jugs into the front of the vehicle. Then the three of us sat side by side in the cab, with Cliff driving. Two hefty young men had climbed into the back, and sat one at each side of the rear door.

There were little knots of spectators at each side of the street as we drove out from the yard. Cliff accelerated rather rapidly, and Stuart and I were thrown sideways as he took two or three corners without slowing.

"Anyone following, Tony?" he called to one of the young men in the back.

"No."

"Good." Cliff eased his pace.

"Somebody might be *following*?" I asked incredulously.

"Can't rule it out," Cliff said. "This is a vanload of food, after all. It's a temptation. That's why we go roundabout ways and keep changing them. And that's why we resprayed the vans to take off the meals-on-wheels sign. We try to be inconspicuous. Nothing to attract attention."

"But . . . surely nobody would steal the old people's dinners," I said.

Cliff and Stuart looked at each other.

"Barry," said Stuart, "it hurts me to break it to you, but there are some around who'd do just that if we gave them a chance."

"Have any of the vans actually been attacked?"

"Not in this city," said Cliff. "Not yet, anyway. But in other places they have. And we've had quite a lot of stuff stolen. That's why we carry a couple of chaps to guard the vans."

I felt disgusted, and said so.

"It's not altogether surprising," Cliff said. "There are millions of people unemployed by now. They're not all that much better off than the old people. The main difference is that they're able-bodied. And when you've got millions of able-bodied men hanging around with no work and not enough to eat—well, it's astonishing that we don't have large-scale riots. I dare say we will have before long. As for stealing from the old folk, it's only a few who'd do that. And hunger's a powerful driving force. Nothing like an empty belly for warping your morality."

"It still sickens me," I said. "We've always looked after old people in this country."

This remark seemed to trigger a sour reaction in Stuart Hazell.

"*Are* we looking after the old people?" he asked.

"Now, now, Stuart, don't get bitter again," Cliff said.

"I can't help getting bitter. It seems to me the government know perfectly well that the old and sick are losing out. They know they can't afford to take up their rations, even if they could find them in the shops. The fact is that there just isn't food for everyone, so the government want the productive workers to get it. That's logical, isn't it? Inhuman but logical. The people still in jobs are keeping things going, maybe even exporting a bit. They have first call on whatever there is."

Stuart's voice was rising as he went on. "What good are old folk?" he asked with fierce sarcasm. "None at all. It's better to have them out of the way. Less mouths to feed!"

"Stuart, Stuart!" Cliff said.

"It's not really as bad as that, is it, Cliff?" I asked anxiously.

"I'm afraid it's not far off," Cliff said. "It's when Stuart gets so furious that he worries me. You see, what I'd like to know is, what else can we do?"

"I'd have thought it was obvious," Stuart said. "Share alike. That's the name of our movement. Puts it in a nutshell. Simple and just."

"Simple to *say*," remarked Cliff.

"Simple to do," retorted Stuart. "The proper thing is for all the food that's produced or comes into the country to be taken over. Otherwise you know what happens to it. It gets into the hands of shopkeepers and black marketeers. They get fat while others get thinner. Well, if the government won't act soon, I know what will happen."

"Don't get going about direct action," Cliff said. "That's wild talk, and you know it. The days of Robin Hood are over. Share Alike can't do anything. It's like the nuclear disarmament people a few years ago. They made all kinds of gestures and got their pictures in the paper, but it didn't have any effect."

"That was different. You're too law-abiding to live in these times, Cliff. And I'll tell you this. I'm meek and mild compared with some of our people. If *I* worry you, you should hear Jim Alsop. He'd scare the pants off you."

"Maybe so. Anyway, we'll have to adjourn the discussion. Barry, this is where our round starts."

We had been driving through an increasingly dingy part of the city, where decrepit factories and warehouses stood cheek-by-jowl with rows of humble, tired old houses. Cliff drew up in front of a terrace house that didn't look as if it had been painted for years.

"Number 17, Signal Street," he said. "Mr. Finnigan. Aged eighty-four. Widower living on his own. Needs soft food because of his teeth."

But Stuart and I were looking farther up the street. Fifty yards along on the other side was a factory entrance. Around it were gathered twenty or thirty men. When the van stopped, they began drifting slowly toward it.

"Benson Engineering," Stuart said. "They closed last week."

"They seem interested in us," I remarked.

"Only the way people are interested in anything that happens, if they've nothing to do," Cliff said reassuringly. "And now that petrol's getting scarce, it's quite an event to have a vehicle come into the street. Well, come on, lads, let's get busy."

We went round to the back of the van. Bill and Tony had opened it up. From one of the metal containers we took a couple of round, flat, lidded tins. Stuart brought two of the big vacuum jugs. By the time everything was ready, a score of people—mostly men, but two or three children as well—had gathered round in a half circle. Though interested enough to come and watch, they looked curiously apathetic; not much talk was going on, and no laughing. They didn't seem hostile. Bill and Tony sat, one on each side of the container, obviously guarding it, and looking embarrassed. But nobody made a move; nobody showed signs of resentment.

Mr. Finnigan sat in his small bare room at a deal table, holding his knife and fork in readiness. Two plates were on the table, and a little heap of notes.

"A good day today, Mr. Finnigan," Cliff said cheerfully. "Mince!"

He decanted a main course onto one of the plates, and some kind of steamed pudding onto the other. Stuart added gravy and custard. There was indeed minced meat as part of the main course: a smallish spoonful of it. The rest looked like carrot and potato. Mr. Finnigan mumbled something that I couldn't understand, but that Cliff interpreted without difficulty. He took the old man's fork and mashed the vegetables up for him. Then he picked up the pile of notes and counted them. "Eighty pounds. Just right," he said. "Well, if you've no problems I'll say good-bye to you, Mr. Finnigan. Somebody'll be round on Friday."

The old man didn't respond. He was single-mindedly shoveling food into his mouth.

"We take their money so that they can keep their self-respect," Cliff said on the way out. "And eighty pounds is quite enough for them to pay out of an old age pension of a thousand a week. But we might as well not bother to take it. It doesn't really help us to pay our way."

"Where does the money come from, then?" I asked.

"It doesn't really. The council say they can't afford to increase our grant from what it was last year. And seeing it's not worth a tenth of what it was, that's just about the same as stopping it. We can't pay the kitchen staff, so they're all volunteers. You can take a turn in there next week."

"And the food itself?"

"We can't pay for that either. We appeal to consciences, hound officials, apply moral blackmail, beg, borrow. . . . We haven't actually had to steal yet."

"It wouldn't be stealing," Stuart said as we got back into the van. His voice was still bitter. "Though I must admit there's not much to be said for keeping Mr. Finnigan going. He's nothing but an old nuisance, a burden. Expendable, that's the word for Mr. Finnigan. He happens to be a living human soul, that's all."

Cliff restarted the engine, cutting into Stuart's voice. We continued the round. By half past one we'd been into the homes of more than thirty people, most of them old and living alone, two or three of them younger but chronically ill. Cliff was professionally cheerful wherever he went, uncannily good at remembering names and showing interest. Stuart, though probably more involved emotionally, was inclined to be abrupt and offhand; you could tell they didn't like him as much.

"A routine kind of day," Cliff said at the end. "Of course, they're the lucky ones. They were on our books before the crisis. They get three meals of a sort every week, and that keeps them going. We haven't taken any new ones on for months. It breaks my heart sometimes to turn them down, but there's nothing we can do."

Three or four times there were little gatherings round the van, but there was never a moment when it seemed as if Bill and Tony would have anything to do. There was one awkward occasion when a distraught young man complained to the heavens that his pregnant wife had more right to be helped than half the people on the list. But the people around were embarrassed and didn't support him. "They're doing their best, aren't they?" one unemployed man said. "Let them get on with it." Cliff gave nothing away at the time, but took the husband's address, and on the way back we called in with a meal that was left over. The young man wasn't grateful. One meal didn't go far, he said, with an undernourished woman who was due to have a baby in a month's time.

Cliff was patient and smiling, Stuart silent. Only as we returned to the van for the last time did I realize from Stuart's drawn white face that he found the whole mission almost unbearably painful. "I think I'll stick to kitchen work if you don't mind, Cliff," he said on the way back to the center. "I suppose I'm feeble, but I just don't have the stomach for going out and seeing what it really means."

Cliff, in the driver's seat, was silent.

"Well, go on," Stuart said. "Tell me I haven't seen anything yet."

"I'm afraid you haven't. But you're wasted, really, on the kitchen work. You're too intelligent. Why don't you join John Reilly on procurement? Persuading people in big organizations that they have stocks or money they can part with. Twisting influential arms, in fact. Do you think you'd be good at that?"

"No," said Stuart. "I'd explode. And Cliff, I don't think it should be a case of begging. I want it to be of right. The greatest good of the greatest number. Share alike."

"I'm a bit surprised you work with us at all," Cliff said.

"Well, a service like this is sharing of a kind," said

Stuart. "So we have to support it. But it doesn't go far. The tip of the iceberg, that's all you touch."

"Too true," Cliff said. "Better that than nothing, though. Now, I hardly need go out of my way to drop you both off at school on the way to the center. Then back to the shop for me, or Barry's dad'll be going hairless. See you both on Friday."

"I suppose so," said Stuart.

I got home late from school that day to find an air of excitement, a superb smell of cooking, and my mother, half apprehensive and half delighted, busy at the stove preparing a special meal. Nessie was helping her.

"It's on account of Mr. Gerald," Mother explained. "He turned up at the shop this afternoon without warning. Your father rang to say they'd both be here for dinner. And this time Mr. Gerald will be staying overnight."

Nessie, who was standing at the sink peeling potatoes, looked at me and pulled a face.

"That'll be a thrill," I said; and then, "I don't think I like Mr. Gerald."

"Nor I," Mother said, surprisingly. "He did nothing for Dad all the years he was in charge, and now he talks about what he *would* have done. And your dad believes him. I think myself he's just after a free meal."

"I can understand that," I said. "It smells good."

"Your father said I could use what I like."

"Then you know about . . . down below?"

"Of course I know."

"So he told you in the end."

"No, he hasn't told me to this day, but he knows I know. How could he do all that without me knowing?"

"Are you making something Ellen likes?" Nessie asked.

"Yes. Roast lamb. I hope she'll eat it."

"I'm worried a lot about Ellen," Nessie said.

Mother sighed. "So am I," she said. "So am I."

Nessie went on, "Since Peggy left, Ellen just seems to have retreated into herself. How often does she talk to you?"

"Not much," Mother told her.

"Nor to me, now I come to think of it," I said.

"No. Nor even to me," said Nessie.

"And she used almost to worship you," I pointed out.

"I think she still does, in a way. But she's withdrawn. I hear her talking to that teddy bear of hers, but as soon as I get within range she stops, so I don't know what she tells it."

"She's off her food, too," Mother said. "Just picks at her meals. Some days she hardly eats a thing."

"Off her food!" I exclaimed. "My goodness, she should see what I've seen today. Off her food, when people are almost starving! That's a joke, isn't it? Except that I'm not laughing."

"She's so thin and pale these days," Mother said. "She's not a happy child at all. I don't know what to do about her. I'm at a loss."

"What's she doing now?"

"At this moment?" Mother said. "She's in her own room. Or she was five minutes ago. She's got all her old dolls out. She's giving them a party."

"Really, Norman," Mr. Gerald said, "I ought to discourage you from entertaining me so generously." He stretched luxuriously in the armchair that was usually Father's and took a sip of brandy. The sitting room was warm, with the gas fire full on and a couple of electric fires giving it help from the sides of the room. The red velvet curtains were comfortably drawn. For once the room seemed welcoming.

"It's a pleasure," my father said. "You know how glad I am to have you here. I only wish you could stay for a while."

"I haven't the least desire for special treatment, you understand. The old days are gone, for better or worse. I'm not your employer now, I'm just a person you happen to know. Just an old widower on his own, without even a housekeeper—my former one has left since I last saw you—or much prospect of getting one in these hard times."

"You aren't just any person to me," said Father, sounding shocked.

"And yet surely you can't treat all your guests like this?" Mr. Gerald said. "I'm sure *I* couldn't."

"We don't have many guests," Father said.

"We don't have *any* guests," said Nessie.

"Quite understandable. The present troubles have made entertaining almost impossible. I appreciate it all the more that you're prepared to let me stay for a time. I shall take you up on that if I may, just for a few days. But I insist that you must offer me only the simplest hospitality, the very simplest. You must let me live as one of the family. That will be privilege enough for me. Will you promise me that, May?"

"What?" said Mother, startled.

"Oh. You're staying?" Father said. He looked just a little surprised, too.

"I hope I didn't misinterpret you, Norman. If so, you must disillusion me. When you said you wished I could

stay, I took you at your word, and felt that a few days
—just a very few days—would be pleasant. But of course,
if it was only a form of words, I shall quite understand."

"It wasn't a form of words," Father said. "What I say I
mean. That's one of my principles. I'll be very glad for
you to stay. It's no trouble having you here. Is it, May?"

"No," said Mother uncertainly.

"Don't worry, I shan't outstay my welcome," Mr.
Gerald said. "But I must say it will be nice to have a
peaceful spell under a friendly roof. I might come on
Monday and stay till the end of the week, if it doesn't
inconvenience anyone too much. And, Norman, I don't
know quite how it is, but your house feels *secure* to me, as
if you were firmly entrenched here. A solid base in an
uncertain world."

"Well, they say an Englishman's home is his castle,"
Father said with some pride.

The phrase "Noah's Castle" came into my mind.

"I must say, it needs to be, in these days," said Mr.
Gerald. His manner, as always, was relaxed. But his eyes
were never sleepy; if one caught a glance from him it was
always a sharp glance.

"I see that a couple of trucks belonging to one of the
supermarket chains were hijacked today," he went on. "I
really don't know what the country's coming to. And I
saw what looked like a street battle on the way over here.
A street battle in broad daylight! I suppose it could have
been some kind of gang war. But the people in it looked
too old for that."

"It's the unemployed," Father said. "Stirred up by
agitators, of course. There's a man in this city called Jim
Alsop who's always causing trouble."

"We're not used to unemployment on the present

123

scale," Mr. Gerald said judiciously. "Perhaps if we'd had it sooner it would have brought people to their senses."

"A charitable thought," said Nessie under her breath to me.

"Anyway," Father said, "the army have been ordered to help the police against rioters. That'll make them toe the line."

"And high time, too," said Mr. Gerald, sipping his brandy again.

"As for this Alsop fellow," Father said, "he gives me the shudders. If you really want to be my enemy, just do anything that'll bring me into contact with him. He ought to be in jail."

"Sounds as if hanging would be too good for him," said Mr. Gerald.

"If you'll excuse me," Nessie said, and she went out. Father stared after her.

"Terry might arrive any time," Mother said by way of explanation. But I had a strong feeling that Nessie had gone because she couldn't stomach what Father and Mr. Gerald were saying.

"Terry is the boyfriend, I assume," Mr. Gerald said. "Is it still serious?"

"Oh, yes," said Mother.

"Not if I know anything about it," said Father. "That Terry's altogether too casual about life. He'll never come to anything. And if you ask me, Nessie knows it. She has sense enough to know which side her bread's buttered on. Mark my words, when it comes to the point she won't leave home till she has somebody who can provide for her as well as I do."

I was astonished that Father should know Nessie so

little. It wasn't her style at all to work out on which side her bread was buttered. But it was Mother who made the practical observation.

"Nessie'll be eighteen a week from today," she said. "Then she'll be of age and she can do as she likes. None of us can stop her."

"We'll see about that," said Father grimly.

"An eighteenth birthday is quite an occasion," said Mr. Gerald. "But difficult to celebrate in present conditions. Norman, we passed the old Theatre Royal on our way here from the shop. Am I right in thinking it's still open?"

"It is, at the moment," Father said. "Though how long it will last I don't know."

"I wondered," Mr. Gerald said, "whether, if she could put up with the company of an old fogy, I might be permitted to take her there as a small birthday treat. That is, of course, Norman, if you had no objection."

"Well, I'd be happy," Father said. "But I suppose her mother is right. She'll be of age in a few days' time, and for better or worse you can't tell these young people what they're to do. Still, it's a very generous suggestion, Gerald. I think you'd better put it to her yourself. I hope she'll accept."

"She generally likes to go out with people her own age," said Geoff bluntly.

For a moment a look of chagrin could be seen on Mr. Gerald's face. It was so fleeting that I was sure nobody else noticed it, and I wouldn't have done so myself if I hadn't been finding Mr. Gerald's face a fascinating study. He was smiling and in full command of himself in an instant.

"Well, it's up to her," he said lightly. "I should be

disappointed, but not the least bit surprised or angry, if she didn't care for the idea. It does of course depend on my being here next Wednesday, but I'm making so bold as to think that will be all right."

"Of course," Father said.

"And it depends on what's on at the theater." Mr. Gerald picked up the evening paper and looked through the advertisements.

"It's *French Without Tears* next week," he said. "The resident company. All week at half past seven."

"That sounds educational," said Father with approval.

"Well, we shall see," Mr. Gerald said. "If I don't get a chance to speak to her before I go, will you put it to her and let me know how she reacts?"

I could tell you now, you old phony, I thought, but I didn't say anything aloud. She'd say, "Nothing doing." Or stronger words to that effect.

"You didn't really mean him to come and stay, did you?" my mother asked my father.

Father looked at her coldly.

"You heard what I told him," he said. "You know me. I say what I mean and I mean what I say."

"But . . . where shall I put him?"

"In the guest room, of course. That's what it's for."

"And what shall I give him?"

"Meals. You heard what he said. He'll be like one of the family. Mr. Gerald's no snob. The simplest hospitality will do for him. Those were his very words."

"But Norman, you looked as surprised as I was when he took you up on it."

"Well . . . All right, I admit, I intended it as a general

expression of feeling toward him rather than an actual invitation. But I'd never say a thing if I wasn't prepared to be taken seriously. That's not me, May. That's not me. Now, it's a real compliment to us that Mr. Gerald is willing to stay with us. I'd never have thought it possible in the old days. Mr. Gerald's a member of a very old business family in this city, very much respected."

"But . . . suppose he finds out about you-know-what?"

"There's no reason why he should find out. Mr. Gerald's not the man to poke his nose into other people's business. I don't suppose he'll set foot in the kitchen, never mind going farther. Just take it easy, May. Give him good but ordinary meals. I'll see that you get what food you need. Don't *fuss* about it."

Mother still looked unhappy but said no more. Father went on, "I hope that girl won't be awkward about going to the theater with him."

"I can tell you right away, she won't go."

"I said she knew which side her bread was buttered on, but sometimes I wonder. You know, Mr. Gerald's a widower. Just now, he hasn't even got a housekeeper. And he's not an elderly man, not by any means. He's only my age. In his prime, in fact. What he needs is to re-marry."

"Why doesn't he, then?" Mother asked.

Father looked at her pityingly.

"Wives suitable for Mr. Gerald don't grow on every tree," he said. "But a girl like Nessie . . ."

"Norman! She wouldn't!"

"She'd be lucky if she had the chance," said Father. "But I admit that's looking ahead a little. Anyway, I'll go up to her room and have a word with her about the theater trip."

"Not now, Norman. Leave it till morning."

" 'Never put off until tomorrow what you can do today,' " Father quoted. "I'll give her as long as possible to get used to the idea. I don't want anyone saying I've sprung it on her."

Mother looked at me in alarm as Father left the kitchen.

"He will go at things like a bull at a gate," she said. "And he ought to know by now that Nessie won't stand for it."

The next minute we heard loudly raised voices from above. Father's, Nessie's, and—surely—Terry's. And two or three minutes after that, Nessie came striding into the kitchen with Father a pace or two behind her. Both were white with fury.

"I will not have you bursting into my room like that!" Nessie declared. "I won't have it! Don't you understand? I'm not a child. I—will—not—have it!"

"Disgusting!" was all Father would say at first. "Disgusting!"

"Not disgusting at all. But not your business, either!"

"While you're under my roof, what you do is my business," Father said, recovering. "And while I'm responsible for what goes on here, it won't include that kind of thing. When I was your age, no decent girl . . ."

"Now, now, Dad," Terry said placatingly. "That was nothing much. No harm in it. You should see what some of them get up to . . ."

Nessie hushed him. "That's not the point," she said. "The point is that a person's room is private. Nobody has any right to push a door open without warning, without so much as a knock. How can I stay in a house where that happens?"

"Nobody has any right to use my house as a . . ." Father began, but swallowed on his final word. "Anyway, it's not *your* room. The house is my house, and the room is part of the house. It's *my* room. *I* shall say what can go on there. And one thing that can't go on there is what you were doing."

Nessie seemed to weary of the argument.

"As Terry says, it was nothing much," she said. "There's no point in discussing it. You needn't think I'm going to say I'm sorry, because I'm not. And the lesson is all too obvious. So why don't we let it drop?"

She turned to Terry.

"Just wait till I get my coat," she said, "and I'll walk halfway home with you. I need to calm down."

But Father wouldn't let things drop. He had gone up to tell Nessie about something, and it was still in his mind.

"It's just as well Mr. Gerald has gone," he said. "I don't know what *he'd* think about it."

"*Mr. Gerald?*" repeated Nessie. "What's it to do with him?"

"You may be interested to know, Agnes," said Father, "that Mr. Gerald has offered to take you to the theater for your birthday."

"Offered to take *me?*" Nessie stared. Then she began to laugh. It was a light, hard laugh, with a growing undertone of hysteria, and it continued long past the point at which any amusement must have ceased.

"Mr. Gerald?" Terry said. "Is that the fat old geezer in the bowler hat and black overcoat who went down the drive a few minutes ago?"

Nessie stopped laughing long enough to say, "Yes," then went on to shake with increasingly helpless laughter. Terry began to laugh with her—not, I thought, of his own accord, but involuntarily, by a kind of contagion.

Father's fury was rising again.

"I won't have you laughing at Mr. Gerald in my house," he said. "I'll have you know that I'm proud of his interest in my family. I won't let anyone mock his generosity."

"His generosity!" Nessie repeated. Suddenly she stopped laughing. A fury was rising in her to match Father's. "I've seen the way Mr. Gerald looks at me," she said. "I know just what he's like. If you think it's all right for me to go out with a dirty old man but all wrong for me to show affection to a young one in my own room, then all I can say is, I'm sorry for you. And sorry for all of us!"

Father was silent for a moment, taken aback by the fierceness of her comment. Nessie gathered her breath for a final pronouncement.

"Shall I tell you how I'm going to celebrate my eighteenth birthday?" she said. "My coming of age? I'm going to celebrate by leaving here and moving over to Terry's. That is, if he and his mum will have me."

Terry beamed.

" 'Course we'll have you," he said. "My mum likes you. Likes anybody, and specially you. That'll be great." He turned to Father. "Sorry, Dad," he said without any sign of resentment. "Hard on you. But that's the way it is. That's how the cookie crumbles. That's life, isn't it? Too bad."

It seemed as if Father would have nothing to say. He was gripping the back of a kitchen chair, his knuckles white. When at last he spoke, it was in a strained, quiet, almost inaudible tone.

"You'll be sorry, girl," he said. "Mark my words, you'll be sorry."

9

MID-FEBRUARY. Snow; the first snow of winter, and quite a lot of it. At Rose Grove the gloomy foliage was hidden under thick white cushions, and the garden seemed brighter than usual. Geoff built a snowman for Ellen in front of the sitting room window. It pleased her, but none of us could get her to go out and play.

Ellen was not the only child who lacked energy to go out and enjoy the snow, although for other children the reason was different. They weren't refusing their food; there was too little food to refuse. Most got by, but few were well nourished. Going around in the snow, you couldn't help realizing that childish high spirits had dipped. On the Mount and in other suburbs there was a notable lack of squeals and laughter, of snowball fights and slides.

Down in the city, snow lay in the streets for a long time. There were no workmen to shift it, because the money in the council's bank account wasn't enough to pay them a living wage. And there weren't enough vehicles around to disperse the snow by simply going about their business. Traffic by now was very limited. There were food delivery trucks, escorted by police on motorcycles; and their arrival at a shop or supermarket would be followed immediately by the formation of a queue. Army vehicles patrolled parts of the city where there were large numbers of unemployed and trouble seemed possible; but so far people were sullen and apathetic, too much occupied with slow and unproductive quests for food to have time for rioting. Ambulances had petrol and were always around, although Cliff and his helpers found it harder and harder to get sick people into hospital.

The rumor was that the old and weak were dying at several times the usual winter rate, but this was hard to substantiate. In fact there were a great many rumors of all kinds around, and nobody knew which ones to believe. The daily papers, unable to get newsprint, had suspended publication. You could buy a four-page news sheet called the *Central Record* at fifty pounds a number, but this was generally regarded as an official mouthpiece and not to be trusted.

Although your eyes and ears told you that things were getting worse, the *Central Record* and the television news bulletins kept on proclaiming that we were about to turn the corner. INFLATION RATE CUT, the *Record* headlines would say, or SUPPLIES IMPROVE, or EXPORTS REVIVE, and there'd be pictures of impressive new machines coming off the production line, or crates being loaded for shipment overseas. There was never anything about the factories that closed down, or the queues that got longer and longer, or the frequent power cuts. Cynicism increased. Our English teacher, after a number of class discussions on the suppression of truth and suggestion of falsehood, based on study of the *Record,* discontinued the series in disgust. The artistic aspect of misleading the public had been abandoned, he said, and now it was sheer brute lying.

At school, attendance was falling, and no real attempt was made to stop truancy. Pupils were occupied in foraging, or in taking their turn to stand for hours in queues. Those who did get to school talked endlessly of food. They'd tell each other about marvelous meals they'd had in the past or were planning to have when the crisis was over. Phrases like "fillet steak" or even "cottage pie" were spoken with as much feeling as if they were poetry. I found this kind of conversation boring. But then, I was all right; I was fit and well fed. Indeed, I began to wonder if my physical well-being was becoming noticeable when so many of those at school with me were growing thin and pale.

I didn't see Wendy Farrar at school, but one morning when I was on my way there I caught sight of her in a queue and passed the time of day with her. She smiled a small wintry smile and gave me no encouragement to go on with the conversation or to visit her house. An inquiry about her mother produced only the three words, "She's all right." Another day, passing a store when the queue happened to be short and I had a couple of hundred pounds in my pocket, I got a can of sardines and left it on the Farrars' kitchen table. If they guessed where it came from, I never knew.

Our meals-on-wheels customers survived, kept going largely by the meager midday dinners we provided; but we knew all too well that for every one on our list there were a score who would have liked to be on it. The old people we fed were aware of their good fortune. They had been bred in hard old times. "I lived through two world wars," was a typical remark, "and I can live through this."

One of the many rumors that went around was that a food truck had been hijacked on its way to the biggest store in our city; and this was probably true, because that day supplies were scarcer and the queue longer than usual. It was said that work was available in the country, helping farmers to guard their livestock against marauders, and moreover that payment was in kind. But those who walked or cycled out of town came back disappointed. Country dwellers would trust only other country dwellers; people who went into the country from the towns were suspected—sometimes with reason—of being up to no good, and were sent packing.

Some events, though not reported in the *Record* or on the news bulletins, did undoubtedly happen. Share Alike held a series of demonstrations in the city center, with banners and shouted slogans. Nobody was arrested; nobody took any notice. The arrival in the main square of a lorry plastered with Share Alike posters and a load of potatoes for free distribution caused more interest. Stuart Hazell was among the helpers who handed out potatoes—one large, two medium-sized, or three small to each applicant while they lasted, and a careful scrutiny to ensure that nobody came round twice. Next day Stuart was triumphant but Cliff was dour. A couple of potatoes in a once-for-all gesture didn't solve anything, he said.

We were still eating well at Rose Grove, though I found my appetite diminishing and a tendency for the food to stick in my throat. When power was cut, Father would run the generator, but he didn't supply us with light that could be seen from outside, for fear of attracting attention.

No more was said about Nessie's impending departure, or about the proposed theater trip with Mr. Gerald. Probably Father accepted that the latter was a nonstarter but hoped that Nessie would quietly drop her intention of leaving home. She didn't. On the morning of her birthday, she didn't appear at the breakfast table. A shout up the stairs to her room brought no response; and when I ran upstairs I found that she was gone already, her bed turned neatly down, and a note on the dressing table that simply said *Sorry*. When Father was told, he sat stony-faced for a minute. Then he said quietly, "She's no daughter of mine," and picked up the *Record*.

Mr. Gerald—informed by Father, I suppose, of the fate of his invitation—put off his visit until a couple of days after Nessie left; and when he came he made no reference to her absence. He arrived with a surprising amount of luggage for a stay of a few days. Geoff and I helped him to unload a trunk, several cases, and a suit carrier. He made himself at home in the guest room and in our sitting room, where he was to be found comfortably installed at most times of the day: apparently dozing, but always—if one spoke to him—sharp and alert. He and Father didn't talk a great deal together; they had nothing in common except recollections of the shoe trade, and that was a limited topic. Mr. Gerald tended to occupy Father's favorite chair, and this, I thought, irritated Father, though he never said anything. Father began staying later at the shop than he'd thought necessary in recent months. He also got into the habit of taking a midevening walk by himself.

Mother would have worried more about the adequacy of her attention to Mr. Gerald if she had been less upset over Ellen. Ellen had now gone right off her food. She would pick at a morsel or two, and when asked if she liked the meal would reply that she did; but when it was over her plate would be almost untouched. Father was annoyed. He seemed to look on Ellen's failure to eat as a kind of perversity, even when she was visibly growing thin and pale. "It's a sin and a shame to waste good food at a time like this," he would say; and Mother would salvage the remnants rather than throw them away.

Eventually Mother took Ellen to see the doctor. She came back as worried as before, and none the wiser.

"He didn't seem to understand," she said. "Kept saying there were thousands in her condition and it was only to be expected. I tried to tell him it was a case of her not wanting to eat, not of there not *being* anything. But he couldn't take it in. 'Whatever there is, you must try to make it appetizing,' he says. 'Children don't understand that they have to eat for self-preservation. I know it's difficult,' he says, 'but you must tempt them.' "

Mother sighed.

"Telling *me* to make it appetizing," she said. "If there's one thing I do know, it's how to cook. Of course, I couldn't say anything to him about . . . about you-know-what, so I suppose he thought we were in the same boat as everyone else. Poor man, he's rushed off his feet anyway. It's surprising he could see us at all."

Suddenly I knew she was near to tears.

"Sometimes I wonder if I'll lose that child," she said. "It seems as if there's nothing I can do for her. And I miss our Nessie. Oh, Barry, love, I do miss Nessie."

"Geoff!" I called. "Geoff?"

There was no reply, and the movement I thought I'd seen, down by the area steps, ceased. I was crossing the gravel at the back of the house, carrying something I'd brought from the garden shed. It was just after dark.

I thought I'd been mistaken in supposing I heard someone, and was on the point of going indoors. Then on impulse I walked round to the area. I could see very little and had no flashlight. But as soon as I reached the top of the area steps I sensed that somebody was there.

"Who is it?" I demanded.

No reply.

There was no room for concealment. I went down the steps and became aware of a small figure, just round the corner from the basement door, pressed flat against the wall. I felt for its shoulders. It thrust a knee in my groin and raced up the steps and away, leaving me writhing and helpless.

Then I heard Geoff's voice and two sets of running footsteps on the gravel. By the time I'd recovered, there was no one near. But I could hear scuffling sounds, and ran toward them.

They were halfway down the drive. Geoff had caught the intruder and was pinning him down.

"Who is it?" I asked again.

"It's Mel Holloway," said Geoff.

"You know what he did? He kneed me."

"The little bastard!"

"I'll . . ." I began. But Mel was helpless, and much smaller than either of us, and I couldn't really start beating him up.

"What were you doing?" Geoff asked him.

"Nothing."

"Mel Holloway," I said, "do you remember that my dad warned you off?"

"Yes," he said.

"Well, now you can come and tell him why you're here again."

"All right," said Mel. And although he was on the ground and firmly held by Geoff, there was still a confident and cheeky note in his voice.

"Wait a minute," said Geoff to me. "Dad's out on his evening walk."

"What shall we do, then?"

"Well . . . Let's get him under the light for a start."

There wasn't a power cut that evening. I went into the house and switched the outside light on. Then Geoff and I held Mel by an arm each, watching his legs carefully. His round, goblinesque face was defiant.

"What have you got?" Geoff asked him.

"Nothing."

That was fairly evident. There was no room on Mel's person for anything of any size, and no reason to suppose he'd been anywhere on our premises where he could have helped himself to small items.

"What," I asked, returning to the key question, "were you doing round the back of our house?"

"I told you. Nothing."

"We're getting nowhere," I said. "We could keep him till Dad comes back, I suppose."

Geoff didn't seem keen on that idea.

"I don't think Dad would get any more out of him than we can," he said. He turned to Mel. "What did you *see?*" he asked.

"See? What did you think I'd see?"

That was dangerous ground, and Geoff went no further on it.

"Listen," he said. "When Dad comes back, I shall tell him we caught you here. And you'll be in trouble, Mel Holloway, and serve you right."

"Think so?" said Mel insolently.

"But just for now, I'm going to let you go. And here's something to take with you, in return for what you did to Barry."

Geoff propelled Mel a few feet down the drive, and sent him on his way by booting him in the backside. This was the first thing either of us had said or done that had any effect. Mel yelped in pain. He went a few yards along the drive, rubbing the injured part, then turned and shouted, "I'll get you, Geoff Mortimer!"

"You and who else?" said Geoff scornfully.

"I'll tell my dad."

"That makes two of us," Geoff called. And, when Mel had gone, "It's just as well Dad didn't see him. He'd have slaughtered him, most likely."

I knew what Geoff meant. Father's control of his temper was uncertain. His reaction to an after-dark prowler, found in so sensitive a place as the area adjoining the basement, might have been violent.

"Actually," Geoff said, "I think Mel was probably just fooling around somewhere he'd no business to be, the way kids do. They're always at it. It doesn't have to mean anything. If it wasn't for the way things are, I don't suppose we'd think anything of it."

We were both thoughtfully silent for a moment or two.

Then Geoff went on, "All the same, I don't like it, do you?"

"I don't like anything about the setup here."

"You like to be able to eat, don't you?"

"Sometimes I even wonder about that."

Geoff looked at me under the porch light.

"Listen, Barry," he said, "whose side are you on?"

"What do you mean, whose side am I on?"

"You know what I mean. Are you backing Dad or not?"

"I don't know, Geoff," I said. "The whole business worries me. You know what things are like. What right have *we* . . .?"

"Dad thought ahead, that's all. The people who complain about hoarders are the ones that didn't think ahead. If *they* were all right, they'd think differently. I can't see that there's anything wrong with planning ahead. In fact, I can't see that Dad's ever done anything wrong. It's not a crime to look after yourself instead of leaving it to other people, is it?"

"Stuart Hazell says that looking after yourself is not enough."

"Oh, Stuart Hazell, you, Nessie, Cliff . . . you all make me sick sometimes. So clever, so well-meaning, and always full of talk while people like Dad and me do the real work."

"But doesn't it bother you when people are ill and hungry?"

"Of course it bothers me. I expect it bothers Dad, too. But he's realistic. He can do something about *us*. He can't do something about *everybody*. And listen, Barry, let me tell you something again, in case it didn't sink in last time.

He's my dad, and I'll stand by him, whatever anyone says. I'll stand by him whatever happens."

One thing Geoff and I agreed on was that Father would have to be told about Mel Holloway's intrusion. The best time to catch him on his own was after the television news, which he always watched. Then he would make some excuse and slip down to the basement for a few minutes, to check that his stores were in order, bring up rations for the following day, and perhaps to enjoy the pleasure of possession. After that he would return to the sitting room for a nightcap with Mr. Gerald, who liked a glass or two of brandy and a little casual conversation before bedtime.

That evening, when it was time for the news, Geoff and I joined Father and Mr. Gerald in front of the television. Ellen, as often happened these days, had gone listlessly to bed in the early evening, and Mother, shy and a little resentful of Mr. Gerald, was sitting by herself in the kitchen.

And as it happened, the news was postponed to make room for a special program launching a government campaign against hoarders.

The Minister of National Recovery, it seemed, was to conduct the campaign in person. The program began with cameras zooming in on the minister and his wife, who were eating an extremely frugal supper of bread and a crumb of cheese. Two or three other couples, described as just ordinary people, were then shown at their equally frugal meals, remarking cheerfully that they were glad to put up with a little hardship for the good of the country.

Then, by contrast, we were shown pictures of several remarkably unpleasant-looking people who'd been convicted of hoarding, followed by shots as mouthwatering as commercials of the food they were said to have stored away. These, said the minister, were the guilty men. These were the ones who drove up prices by creating artificial scarcity. These were to blame, rather than poor crops, or the need of backward countries to keep their food for themselves, or the incompetence of governments, or industrial inefficiency, or labor disputes, or ill-understood economic forces. These, the hoarders, were the public enemy. At this point, cartoon-style drawings were shown of characters even more villainous and miserly-looking than the real people whose portraits we'd seen, clutching piles of goodies to themselves.

The minister reappeared for a moment. "Is *your* neighbor a hoarder?" he inquired. Cartoon pictures followed of an innocuous, friendly-looking male neighbor in a bowler hat and of a female neighbor in housewife's apron. Then their faces changed into the villainous, miserly ones of the previous drawings. And their garages, garden sheds, and spare rooms were shown with their walls bulging out and pulsing with all the things you couldn't get in the shops.

"If you have reason to think *your* neighbor is a hoarder," the minister urged viewers earnestly, "don't let friendly feelings get in the way of your public duty. Tell the police. You owe it to yourself and to your country. Your information will be treated in confidence. Nobody will ever know. So *tell the police*. Good night."

The rest of the news was cut down to half a dozen quick-fire items, and was over in a couple of minutes.

To me the campaign had rather a phony ring. It seemed as if the government was trying to divert attention from the real problems, and its own failure to solve them, by holding up this dummy figure of the Hoarder for the public to hate. Yet all the same it was immensely alarming to realize that my own father was among the objects of such a ferocious attack. When Father leaned forward to switch the set off, I knew that the program had had its effect. Not that his hands trembled, or that there was any outward sign of nervousness that a casual eye would have noticed. It was only that, knowing Father well, I could sense the tightly controlled tension in his movements. I could see Mr. Gerald watching him as well. And I suspected that there was nothing of the casual observer about Mr. Gerald.

"Well," Mr. Gerald said now, "that was all a ridiculous exaggeration. But I must say that if I were sitting on vast stores of everything, I should be quaking with terror. To think that an unguarded word or a touch of neighborly malice might get one branded as a public enemy and probably sent to jail. Wouldn't that worry *you*, Norman?"

"What?" said Father. "Yes. Yes, I suppose so."

"For better or worse," Mr. Gerald went on, "that's one crime that nobody could find *me* guilty of. My cupboard at home has all too much in common with that of the late lamented Mother Hubbard."

"What?" said Father again; and then, "Oh, yes."

"In fact," said Mr. Gerald, "there is danger that even quite innocent people, who just happen to have a *little* put by through normal foresight, and who maybe manage to get their full rations when others don't, might be denounced. That would be dreadful. It really does make one think of the police state. The knock in the night that we used to be always hearing about."

"Yes," said Father.

"Somebody like yourself, even, Norman. I'm sure you would never be a hoarder. That wouldn't be like the Norman Mortimer I've known and respected for so long. But suppose some ill-intentioned person—perhaps some neighbor whom you might have asked into your house out of the kindness of your heart, and given the best of what you had at the expense of your own future menu —suppose some such dreadful person were to report you, and you had the police coming round . . ."

I could feel that with each successive sentence he was winding up the tension in Father. At some point it might snap. That could be disastrous. Actually Father kept control remarkably well. But I saw, and perhaps Mr. Gerald also saw, that his fists were clenched and his fingernails digging into his palms.

"Supposing somebody was jealous because you and your family look better fed than the majority?" Mr. Gerald went on. "One never knows what people will stoop to. . . . However, I mustn't raise such alarming specters. I'm sure your friends and neighbors are the nicest, most reasonable people, quite unlikely to want to get you into trouble. And of course, Norman, *I* know that you couldn't have anything to hide."

"If you'll excuse me, Gerald," said Father, in a steady and level voice—maintained, I suspected, with enormous effort—"I must just go and see to a small job that needs doing in the kitchen. Let me pour you a drink before I go."

He poured out brandy with a steady hand and passed the glass to Mr. Gerald, who received it gracefully.

"You treat me so well, Norman," he said. "So very well. I really do appreciate it. I should so hate anything unpleasant to happen."

Geoff and I gave Father two or three minutes' start. Then we slipped away from the sitting room in turn. I was the second to go. I left Mr. Gerald contentedly arranged in Father's chair, flicking idly through a travel book, his glass at hand on a low table: a plump, comfortable cuckoo in our nest.

Down in the basement, Father was sitting on a kitchen chair at his battered old desk, and Geoff was already telling him about the capture of Mel. Neither of them looked toward me as I approached. Father listened with a set face and without comment. When Geoff had finished, he asked, "Could he have seen anything?"

"I wouldn't have thought so," Geoff said. "Would you, Barry?"

"No," I said. "It was dark, the windows are curtained anyway, and I'm sure he didn't get inside. And we don't absolutely *know* that he was snooping. As Geoff said, kids are always up to tricks of one kind or another. It may not mean anything at all."

"He might have been hoping for a sight of Ellen," Geoff said. "He might be sweet on her."

"Doesn't seem too likely," I said. "He's about twelve and she's ten. He'd be more likely to be sweet on Nessie."

Father wasn't interested in this kind of speculation.

"I wish it hadn't happened," he said. "We don't know

how many times the lad may have been skulking around here without being caught. And I don't trust these Holloways. I know Mel's dad, Vince Holloway, through business contacts. He's a real crook."

"According to the Minister of Whatnot, *you're* a crook," said Geoff.

I wouldn't have dared to say that to Father at any time, but Geoff—never sensitive—came out with it quite casually.

Father flinched, but his answer was calm.

"I don't take my morality from those fellows," he said. "I know what's right. I shall look after those who depend on me. I don't reproach myself for that." He paused.

"All the same," he went on, "it's a worry. I wouldn't have thought it would be so hard to keep a thing to ourselves."

"Do you trust Mr. Gerald?" I asked.

Father stared.

"I mean," I said, "that he seemed to be hinting at something. In fact, it was rather obvious, wasn't it?"

"No, no," said Father. "Mr. Gerald's a very straightforward gentleman. He just said what came into his head after seeing that broadcast. I admit it cut a bit near the bone. In fact, to tell you the truth, it upset me for a minute or two. I did just wonder if he'd noticed something. But I don't think he can have done. Not that I think there'd be real harm in it if he did. I mean, can you imagine Mr. Gerald giving me away? Mr. *Gerald?*"

"I don't know quite what I could imagine about Mr. Gerald," I said. "But I'm sure there are no flies on him."

"Well, I'll tell you something," Father said. "I've

started on this course of action and I'm going to stick it out. And I'm trusting you two. I have to trust you, haven't I? And I know I can."

He put a hand out to each of us, his right to Geoff, his left to me. I had a sudden urge to draw my hand away. But I couldn't bring myself to do so.

"Well," Father said, "I'd better get back to Mr. Gerald, or he *will* be beginning to think I'm up to something. And if you two have finished your homework, why don't you go to bed? Too many late nights, that's what's wrong with you young folk these days."

This last remark was automatic; I'd heard him make it scores of times before. He yawned. I wasn't feeling tired at all, but it came over me that Father, after months of work and strain, was very tired indeed.

I slept later than usual next morning, and was awakened by the sound of shots. One, two, three of them. I went to the window and looked out over the back lawn. Standing on a box was a little row of tin cans. As I watched, a fourth shot cracked out. A can jumped from the box and spun away toward the rhododendrons.

10

LATE FEBRUARY: the snow almost gone, though lingering in the lee of hedges and in other shaded spots. The first of my two weekly days at the center was one of those that always come toward the end of February, when the air is fresh and mild, and spring seems for the moment to be within touching distance. In the gardens on the Mount, retreating snow had uncovered a scatter of green bulb shoots. Even Rose Grove had a crocus or two to show. Against all odds I felt a joy in the returning season spring up in myself.

At the center the queue seemed longer, and built up earlier, than ever. Better weather had brought out scores of old folk, not on the list for home visits, who saw the prospect of a meal. By half past ten, Mike had gone out to station himself at the back of the line and turn away new arrivals.

Walking past the queue of people, none of whom would wait less than an hour and a half before being skimpily fed, I felt my elation seeping away. And when I got to Cliff's tiny office at the back of the center the last traces of it vanished. Cliff was in a state of mingled fury and heartbreak. One of his teams had been embezzling two or three meals on each round; they set out with sufficient on board, but somehow they didn't have quite enough to complete the circuit. As they made sure that different customers went short each time, this could have continued for quite a while without much risk of detection, if one member hadn't had pangs of conscience and given the game away. Cliff had spoken sternly to the team leader, who was also the driver, but hadn't sacked him. Help was scarce and the teams were unpaid. Cliff thought a warning would serve.

Next day the team leader had driven the loaded van away from the center and had been seen no more.

Cliff was almost in tears. It wasn't so much the loss of the van, which would probably be found abandoned somewhere, or even the loss of the food; it was the disillusionment with human nature.

He was in for a further shock that afternoon, when he ran me back to school after I'd finished a stint in the kitchen.

In Sunderland Street, a narrow and slightly run-down street in a secondary shopping area of the city, we were held up by a press of people. Most of them appeared to be sightseers. The center of attention was a grocery store of which the plate glass window had been knocked in, leaving only a jagged fringe around the edge. There was glass everywhere, and half a dozen bricks lay on the pavement. Inside, something like a free fight was going on, as more people struggled to get in than the limited floor space would hold. Others were forcing their way out, laden with cans, jars, bottles, and loose packets of food. It all came, apparently, from an inner room. As we watched we saw two men, separately, come round the corner, stare at the scene, then push their way in through the crowd to get what they could. No police were in sight.

"There's Stuart!" Cliff exclaimed. "And Jim Alsop! Stuart! Jim!"

Stuart was standing on the fringe of the crowd with a youngish, tall, red-bearded man. They heard us at the second call and came across. As they approached, Jim clasped his hands and raised them in a boxer's gesture of triumph.

"How's that?" he yelled. "Isn't that great?"

Stuart looked uncertain. Cliff was horrified.

"What's great?"

"Direct action!" shouted Jim.

"My God!" said Cliff.

The car was still held up. The crowd on the pavement and in the street was trying to make space round somebody who'd fainted or been knocked over and was being trampled on. Somebody else was bleeding from a cut on a sharp edge of glass.

"Great?" Cliff repeated. And then, in anger, *"Great?"*

"It's Hudson's," Jim said. "He's a cheat, a twister, a black marketeer. Oh boy, does he deserve this!"

"It's not a Share Alike effort, is it?" Cliff asked.

"You bet it is!" Jim was exultant. "We brought the leaders down here. We organized it. Old Hudson had it coming to him, and we made sure it came!"

"Hey, Jim, careful what you say!" Stuart warned him.

"You think I'm ashamed?"

"No, but . . ."

Cliff said, "I don't think much of looting. Or the kind of scrum that's going on now. Or people getting hurt."

"Nor I!" said Stuart unexpectedly. "That's not what

151

Share Alike is about. Another time, we'll have to organize a proper distribution."

"If you can!" Cliff said dourly.

Jim Alsop was unaffected by any of this. He clasped his hands and waved them high again.

Behind us, three or four more vehicles were held up. Now they began to hoot. Reluctantly Cliff let in the clutch and began to nose his way gently through the crowd.

"You know what?" he shouted to Jim and Stuart through the open window as the car moved away. "You're playing straight into the government's hands!"

There was no response. The two were heading back toward the shop. Looters milled around, many of them coming out with their arms full and hurrying away up side streets. Others had shopping carts. One man arrived with a wheelbarrow as we left.

Cliff, furious by now, halted the car again.

"Why do you think the police don't come?" he yelled after Stuart and Jim. But they didn't turn round. Behind us, two or three cars hooted. Cliff let in the clutch once more, crawled for a few yards, then was through the mass of people and had a clear road ahead. He sighed.

"Jim Alsop's a madman," he said. "You could expect anything from him. But I'd have thought Stuart would have more sense. What do they think will be achieved by that kind of thing? Do you see it as a useful piece of redistribution, Barry?"

"No. Nor does Stuart, I think, now he's seen what happens."

"And nor do I. All it does is make things that used to be unthinkable more and more thinkable. Every raid of that kind makes the next one more likely. And if law and order break down . . ."

Cliff paused as he negotiated an awkward turn, then went on without finishing the sentence.

"Jim Alsop would be glad if it did. Glad for a while, anyway. Well, here we are, Barry. I'll drop you at the end of the school drive."

I was about to get out of the car when Cliff said in an embarrassed tone, "How's Nessie these days?"

"Oh, fine."

"A long time since I saw her. Is she still going out with that tall, fair boy?"

"Terry? Oh, yes."

I didn't tell Cliff that Nessie had moved into Terry's house. Some of his views were conventional, and I thought he might be shocked. As it was, he sighed, and dropped the subject.

"High time I was back at work," he said. "I can't stay late tonight to make up. I must go out looking for lodgings. My present ones aren't nice at all, but good ones are hard to find. It's a dreary business, living in digs, Barry. Oh, well, I mustn't complain. There are lots of people far worse off than me, and don't I know it!"

I got out of the car and turned to close the door. By now Cliff's thoughts had evidently gone back to the default of the team leader and the riot we'd witnessed.

"Funny kind of day it's been, hasn't it, Barry?" he said. But he wasn't laughing.

In its edition for our city next morning, the *Record* ran quite a big local-page story about the raid on Hudson's

Stores. It didn't say anything about Share Alike, or about looting, or about the fact that people had been hurt. The whole incident, it appeared from the *Record,* was a spontaneous outburst of public indignation after Mr. Hudson had been fined for illicit deals in food.

A local-page editorial remarked sanctimoniously that it couldn't condone the crowd's behavior but that this should serve as a warning to anybody who might still be breaking the rationing or hoarding regulations. If honest citizens were driven to take the law into their own hands, it concluded, those who had provoked them could hardly expect the protection of the police.

"I thought he was only staying for a week," Mother said.

"That's right," Father told her.

"Well, he's been here more than a week already."

"Oh? Do you have to count the days, May?"

"I'm only telling you. Ten days ago today he arrived. And he hasn't said anything to *me* about leaving. I wondered if he'd said anything to you. That's all."

"Well, he hasn't. And if you think I'm going to drop hints, you've got another think coming. Listen, May, it's a privilege to have Mr. Gerald here. He'll go in his own good time, and as he said he'd only be here for a week, I expect it will be pretty soon. But I'm not pushing him out."

"No," Mother said. And groused to me, half under her breath, "Your father keeps that treatment for his own family."

"What?" said Father. "What was that, May?"

"Nothing."

"If you've something to say, don't mumble. Let me hear it."

"I was saying," Mother said clearly, "that I do miss our Nessie."

Father's face froze.

"I'll thank you," he said, "not to mention that girl's name in front of me."

"Barry!"

She came up to me out of the shadows as I left our drive; a small, slight figure.

"Hello, Wendy. I haven't seen you for a while."

"No. I haven't been going to school."

"You've been all right?"

"Oh, yes, *I've* been all right. Been busy standing in queues, that's all. I'm not the only one."

I waited, knowing she wanted to ask me something.

"Barry!"

"Yes?"

"I don't know how to say this. I swore I never would."

"Go on. Say it."

"Barry, she's so *weak*. I can't get anything to nourish her, I just can't. This week it's not so much a matter of queuing, it's a matter of paying for what you can get. Do you know how much a loaf of bread costs?"

"A thousand pounds?"

"That was last week's price. It's two thousand five hundred today. Tomorrow it'll be up again. It's more than our week's income. And the baker doesn't really want to sell his bread for money anyway."

"Could you *bake* bread?"

"There hasn't been flour for weeks. I got a loaf yesterday, and the promise of another tomorrow, in exchange for the sitting room clock. But there isn't much we can part with, Barry. I've traded most of the crockery for food already. There's always a demand for pots, because people can't replace their breakages. I can't let the bedding go; I need it to keep her warm. And nobody would want our furniture. I'm chopping that up to burn in her grate when the power cuts are on."

"Oh, my God."

"I suppose if I was one kind of girl I could get something. You can guess how. But there's plenty of girls on the market. You can have a girl for a can of beans, they say. I couldn't compete."

"Wendy, are you asking me to help?"

"Yes, if you can. I'm so ashamed, Barry. I just hated taking stuff from you before. I felt as if I'd never be able to look you in the face again. You can't guess how I feel now, you just can't imagine how awful. I wouldn't do this for anything else in the world. But she's my mother, and she might be . . ." Wendy didn't finish that sentence. "She's so thin and weak, she has no reserves. She might, honestly she might . . ."

"Why do you think I can help?"

She didn't answer that. She looked me full in the eyes and asked another question.

"Can you?" she said.

"I . . . don't know. I wish I knew why you think I can."

"Well, there was what Ellen took to the party, and what you brought to me. I thought there was just a chance that you might still have something. I'd pay you back when the crisis is over."

"I'm sorry," I said, "but I don't think there's anything more I can bring you."

"All right, Barry. It was too much to hope for, I know." She made as if to leave me.

"Wait a minute," I said. "Let me think."

I didn't know how to go on. The thought of letting somebody know we had supplies was a worrying one, to say nothing of the question of whether I could draw on them. Not that I'd made any promise of secrecy to Father. Not that this girl was likely to tell anyone. Not that there weren't a few potential security leaks already. But still . . .

"I don't want anything for myself," Wendy said. "I'm perfectly all right. I'm stronger than I look. It's for her. Oh, Barry, if you could see her . . . But I wouldn't want you to. If I could just find a way of getting, say, some soup powders and meat cubes, and maybe some dried milk, it would help me to see her through."

"I'll see what I can do," I said heavily. "There *could* just be something still around."

She wasn't elated. She could sense that I was reluctant as well as uncertain.

"Of course I couldn't take it if it was going to mean any of *you* going short."

"No, it wouldn't mean that," I said. "Look, I'm not promising, but if I can get something I'll bring it along tomorrow. If I can't, well, I'm sorry."

"I'll be grateful to you as long as I live anyway."

But I didn't want her gratitude. I felt a strange, illogical resentment. She had brought the deepest terror of the present situation too close to me, and it was hard to bear. And at the same time I felt a return of the painful surge of loyalty to Father that I'd experienced while filling my rucksack in the basement three or four weeks before. I didn't want to do anything that seemed like acting against him.

With resentment on my side and embarrassment on hers, there was no ease between us. We walked side by side along the road, not speaking. At the next turning Wendy said, "This is my way. I'd better go home and see how she is."

"All right."

"Good-bye, Barry." This in a very quiet voice.

"Good-bye. See you."

She went. I was pretty sure she was crying.

"Mr. Gerald . . ." Mother began.

Mr. Gerald put down the *Record* and got up courteously from Father's armchair.

"Just Gerald, please, May," he said. "I really feel those old styles of address are better dropped, don't you? We're all equals these days."

"Gerald," Mother began again, and paused, embarrassed.

"Yes?"

"I wondered . . ." She paused yet again. Mr. Gerald waited patiently for her to continue. I had a feeling that he knew just what she wanted to say, and his smiling encouragement was designed to increase her embarrassment.

"I wondered," she said at last, "whether you'd decided how long you're going to stay with us."

"Why, do you want the room for somebody else?" Mr. Gerald asked, still smiling.

"Er—no."

"Then perhaps the pleasure of my company has worn off?"

"Oh, no, not that," Mother said.

"Perhaps I've outstayed my welcome." He was smiling still. "That would never do, May."

"I don't mean that, Mr.—I don't mean that, Gerald. It's just that . . . well, running a house these days is a bit difficult, and it does help me if I *know* things."

"So you want to know when I'm going."

Mr. Gerald sat down again in Father's chair.

"Do take a seat, May," he said. He spoke as if he were the host and Mother a nervous, awkward guest.

"You know," he said, "I really am very comfortable indeed here. I appreciate the way you look after me. I haven't been as well cared for since my poor wife passed away."

"Thank you," Mother said.

"It's a great contrast with my own rather cheerless house, especially since my housekeeper left."

Mother said nothing to that.

"So it hurts me a little to think that I may not be welcome here."

"I didn't say that," Mother pointed out.

"No. Quite true. However . . . Oh, here comes Norman, back from the shop already. You've had a good day, I hope, Norman?"

"As good as can be expected these days," Father said.

"May was just wondering when I plan to leave," said Mr. Gerald.

"May!" Father was instantly furious. "Didn't I tell you . . .?"

"There, Norman, don't be cross," said Mr. Gerald. "A

natural question, after all. A woman wants to know what is going on in her realm."

"Her realm!" repeated Father. I could have told Mr. Gerald that he regarded the whole house as his realm and nobody else's.

"But I was just saying, I'm extraordinarily comfortable here. Of course I wouldn't wish to cause trouble to anyone. But it has crossed my mind . . . You know, I do wonder whether, if I were not too great a burden, I might be able to stay a little longer. Until the bad weather is over, perhaps. I realize that the suggestion may seem a little impertinent, coming from me. I can only hope you'll take it as the sincerest compliment I could pay to your hospitality. Of course I should insist on making some contribution to the household expenses."

It wouldn't have taken as observant a man as Mr. Gerald to see what effect this suggestion had on Mother. Her face fell, beyond any hope she could have had of concealment.

"Well!" she said.

Even Father looked somewhat taken aback.

"I . . . hadn't really considered that possibility," he said slowly.

"I hope it doesn't strike you as an alarming one," Mr. Gerald said.

"No, of course not. But . . ."

A pause. Mr. Gerald was at ease and still smiling.

"Perhaps we could just try it and see how we get on," he suggested.

"We . . . well, our usual way of life, especially in these times, isn't what you're used to," Father said. "It isn't even what you've seen in the past week or so. It's rather frugal, I'm afraid." He spoke without his usual briskness, almost as if he were making time for himself to think.

"That's understood, Norman. Few people in these days can live as well as we have all been doing. I'm very well aware of that, Norman. Very well aware of it indeed."

Father seemed now to have made his mind up.

"It's a nice idea, Gerald," he said. "I'm glad that you've felt comfortable enough to suggest it. It's been an honor for me to have you staying here. I could hardly have imagined it in the old days. But—well, these *are* difficult times, and very worrying for May, especially as her health hasn't been good."

Mother stared at this. Though she was thin and straight and had never looked blooming with health, she was in fact never ill and rarely off color.

"I'm not sure that she could manage it, Gerald," Father went on. "I'm not sure that we ought to ask her to."

That must have surprised her no less. Father wasn't usually so considerate.

"So I think perhaps better not. Of course, there's no hurry, and if it would suit you to stay a few days more, that's all right. I'd be glad of that. But perhaps before *too* long . . ."

At last Mr. Gerald stopped smiling, but only for a moment. He rearranged himself neatly in the armchair. Then he said, "There are some advantages in my being here, Norman."

Father looked at him questioningly.

"I have a high opinion of you, Norman, as you know. I think of you as an old colleague. As an old friend, if I may say so. I should hate to see you get into any difficulty."

"Difficulty?" said Father.

"Do you remember that program we saw on television the other night, Norman? When that dreadful man, the minister for something improbable, was encouraging people to inform on their neighbors?"

"Yes," said Father shortly.

"It crossed my mind that you could be vulnerable to some such action."

"Oh!" said Father. His face went white. I saw his hands clench and unclench. Then he looked across at me. I was in the corner of the sitting room where I usually took my homework, and up to this point it seemed as if nobody had really noticed my presence; it was so ordinary. But now Father said, "Barry!"

"Yes, Dad?" I said brightly, looking up.

"I'll ask you to leave us for a while. You could work in your bedroom."

"There's another hour before your meal's ready," Mother added.

I gathered my books and papers together and went out of the room. As I closed the door I heard Father say, in a hard voice he had never used to Mr. Gerald before, "And just what do you mean by that?"

After supper I helped Mother wash the dishes. She was thin-lipped and withdrawn, with little to say. Eventually I asked her outright. "When will Mr. Gerald be leaving?"

Mother gave me, for her, an unusually sharp look.

"I don't know," she said. "There's no date fixed. He's staying for a while to see how we get on."

I took a deep breath and asked another question, realizing that I risked being rebuked.

162

"Was he really threatening to give us away?"

Mother seemed ready enough to answer.

"If you ask me, he was. When your dad taxed him with it, he denied it. Said he only had in mind that there might be malicious gossip, and if anybody got any wrong ideas he'd put them right. And that anyway he'd only been hoping we'd let him stay on a bit until he got his own household sorted out. Smooth he was, you might say smarmy. It seemed to me it was a case of a wink being as good as a nod. There was a message, and your dad got it. But if he did, he didn't let on, he just said Mr. Gerald could stay for a while. They finished up being as nice as pie to each other. Of course, your dad always thought the world of Mr. Gerald. What he really thinks now I don't know, and probably I never shall. He doesn't confide in me."

Mother paused. Then she said fiercely, "I'll tell you one thing, Barry. If that man doesn't go before long, I will."

For a while the clash between my parents and Mr. Gerald put out of my mind the problem of Wendy's mother. But as the evening went on, it returned. I knew I had no choice; I had to try to get food for her. After all, if I had understood Wendy correctly, it was a matter of life and death. The question was how to do it.

The easiest way, undoubtedly, was theft. Although Father checked his stores regularly, he couldn't check every single item every night. If I chose my time carefully I could avoid being caught and I could take things that he wouldn't miss for a while. But my previous encounter with Father in the basement had disturbed me in various ways, and I felt a strong reluctance to take from him without telling.

Another possibility was to tell him frankly what I was doing and defy him to stop me. I didn't care for that thought, either. I'd defied him once before for the same purpose, but that was on the spur of the moment. I didn't know whether I could do it deliberately, or even whether I should.

The best thing I could think of was to put it to Father openly and ask him to help. I didn't suppose he would do so out of sympathy for Wendy and her mother; he didn't even know them. But we were on good terms at present. He might just do it because I was his son and I wanted it.

I found him in the sitting room on his own. Mr. Gerald, perhaps finding the atmosphere too tense after the clash, had said he was tired and had gone to his room. Father was looking harassed, and I felt some doubt about putting my request to him. But perhaps it was the right moment, for he was glad to see me and seemed to be in a sympathetic frame of mind. And Nessie's departure seemed to have produced a slight change in his views on helping people outside the family.

"Does this girl mean something to you?" he asked after I'd spelled out Wendy's need.

"I suppose so. At least, I *know* her and her mother, and I don't like to think of them being in such bad trouble as this."

"You're too young to be serious about a girl," Father said. (I'd expected that; it was his standard line.) "But all the same, if this one's some kind of friend, if you have feelings for her, I'll treat her right. That sister of yours was foolish, you see."

It was the first time he'd mentioned Nessie in my hearing since the day she left.

"If she'd got her young man accepted in the family," he said, "I'd have looked after him, just like ourselves. Of course, that Terry wasn't what I'd have chosen for her, but if they'd played their cards right I'd have accepted him. As it is, she's cut herself off. . . . If you see her, Barry, try to make clear to her what she's done. And tell her it could still be undone."

I wondered whether Father thought that what he himself had done could be undone. But it would never enter Father's head that he could be wrong. I didn't say anything, and a moment later he went on, "Now, go and get your bag, and we'll see what we can find."

On the way down to the basement he asked me a few questions about Wendy. I gave what replies I could.

"She sounds harmless," he said at length. "I might well let you bring her home sometime. But don't tell her anything about all this."

"Don't worry, I won't."

"Are these the same people you took stuff for before?"

"Yes."

"You know," Father said, "what they need is somebody in the house who's at work, and whose earnings go up with the cost of living. Have they thought of taking a lodger?"

And on this prompting, the splendid thought came to me. Yes, why shouldn't they take a lodger? I knew somebody steady and responsible who'd been complaining about his present place. "That's a great idea," I said. "I'll pass it on."

On the way back upstairs with the loaded rucksack,

Father showed slight signs of regretting his generosity.

"You needn't think," he said, "that this means I'm going to dish out for all and sundry. Or for the same people again and again. You realize that, Barry, don't you? This is a special case. A very special case."

I put the things I'd brought on the Farrars' kitchen table. Once again Wendy's embarrassment was painful.

"I kept a list of everything you gave us before," she said. "I'll do the same with this. And I'll see that you get it all back some day. That's a promise. But by then of course it won't be as important. We can't ever repay you, really."

"I've got a good idea for you," I said. "It came from my dad. Why don't you take a lodger?"

"A lodger?" She looked uncertain. "I suppose we could. But isn't it a bit risky in these times? You hear such a lot of stories just now about lodgers who attack or steal from the families they're with. Not that we've much to steal. . . ."

"I have the ideal lodger in mind," I said. "Guaranteed not to attack or steal from anybody. As nice a person as you could wish. Goes by the name of Trent. Clifford Trent."

11

THE BEGINNING OF MARCH; and as so often the appearance of spring in February had turned out to be a mirage. We could well have been back in January now. There was a succession of bitter, iron gray midwintry days when the Mount, though in truth no more than a slightly elevated suburb, felt high and bleak and exposed; and down in the hard, leafless city gray skies met gray roofs, and gray people struggled, with collars turned up, along gray streets.

The number of looting raids was growing. Cliff had said that each successful raid made others more likely, and there was every reason to think he was right. So far, the government wasn't trying too hard to discourage mob action against individuals. Probably casual lawlessness was seen as less dangerous than more organized forms of violence. The official line in news bulletins and the *Record* was that the victims of attack were hoarders or profiteers, and that it served them right. Posters indeed had been put up everywhere denouncing the Hoarder and the Profiteer, shown as a thin miserly figure and a pot-bellied gloating figure respectively.

In the public mind it seemed that both figures were

identified with the small shopkeeper. It was generally believed that the big supermarkets were dealing fairly. If you queued for long enough, and if they got any deliveries, they would sell you what they had at the controlled price. Probably most small shopkeepers traded fairly, too. But undoubtedly there were some shops where very little business was done over the counter.

The temptations to under-the-counter dealing were great, because controlled prices hadn't increased at anything like the same rate as the amount of money there was around. Wages were now paid daily, and people who were lucky enough to be in work and to belong to strong unions were getting raises based on the foreign exchange rates. As our currency went down, their wages automatically went up. And since the arrival of rations was uncertain anyway, it was all too easy for an unscrupulous shopkeeper to hold them back from an old person with only a few thousand pounds in his purse, in order to sell them later in the day on the black market to somebody who could pay as many tens of thousands as the old person could pay single thousands.

Not that anyone was much impressed by tens or even hundreds of thousands of pounds. The story went round our city, and was quite probably true, of the housewife who'd put down a shopping bag stuffed with notes and had come back to find the notes blowing around the street but the shopping bag stolen. A shopping bag was worth more than money. And a lot of business was said to be done in the back rooms of shops by people who had goods of their own to dispose of, or household equipment to sell, or (most desired of all) foreign currency.

There'd been a split in Share Alike. In our city the

main body of the movement, to which Stuart Hazell belonged, had finally decided against violence, and was campaigning for fair shares by means of peaceful demonstration and voluntary effort. But a militant wing led by Jim Alsop was scornful of such methods, and had broken away. It called itself Share Now. Its members were organizing what they called direct action, usually meaning raids on shops. It was alleged that the militants were acting from political motives, but this was hard to prove or disprove, especially when there was no independent press or radio comment. Certainly raids and riots became easier to organize as people grew hungrier and unemployment increased.

It was the first Friday of March when the row of shops on the way down from the Mount to the city was raided. This was a big raid, carried out early in the day. And it was a much more subtle operation than the one against Hudson's Stores. No windows were broken. The raiders entered each shop by the door, bound and silenced the shopkeeper, and passed out what they could find to a row of waiting vans.

Fred Birkett, the greengrocer at the end of the row, had little to lose except the fruit and vegetables he'd been able to buy in the market an hour or two earlier, but he got a nasty blow on the head while trying to resist. Margaret's babywear shop next door was cleaned out; babywear could always be bartered. Mr. Spence the grocer lost all his stock, and was bitter about it; his stock, he said, was all he had in the world, and he didn't have the millions of pounds he'd need to replace it. He was insured for fifteen hundred pounds, which wouldn't buy a box of matches. Mr. Allen, the confectioner next door to him, turned out to have a good deal of food and drink in store that presumably had been acquired in swapping deals with other shopkeepers. That all went, and Mr. Allen had the good sense not to complain. Oddly enough, the one undoubted profiteer in the row, Mr. Turp the butcher, lost hardly anything. It seemed that he had been tipped off. The amount of meat on sale was small and the cold store empty, and there was no sign of any accumulation of goods in the back of the shop or in the flat above. Next day Mr. Turp was smiling again.

At the welfare center, the line of old people waiting for meals dwindled, as was usual in cold weather. It was just as well, because in spite of constant efforts to get supplies, the number of meals that could be produced was shrinking all the time. Cliff believed that many of the usual customers were staying in bed, trying to keep warm. There were more and more power cuts, but nothing was said about them in the news bulletins or the *Record,* so nobody knew whether they were caused by strikes or by lack of supplies. To many old people it made no difference; they couldn't afford to use electricity anyway.

Dying of cold—hypothermia was the fancy name for it—was believed to be common among old people, but once again there was a lack of reliable news. What was passed from mouth to mouth was either rumor or secondhand information from people who happened to know people. But doctors, ambulance men, and undertakers were among those who could still get petrol. Hospitals were crowded and had stopped all visiting; you couldn't get into one without a doctor's recommendation, and it had to be for something pretty serious.

At school there was a dramatic but short-lived improvement in the midday dinner, when the school pigs, formerly fed largely on swill from the kitchen and dining room, were destroyed. There wasn't any swill for them any more. ("All animals are equal," said our witty English teacher, "but some are less equal than others.") For two or three days, everyone who could scrape a few thousand pounds together came in for dinner. The pigs had had names, and there was speculation among those acquainted with them as to whether today's portions came from Percy, Alfred, or Douglas. Then it was all over, and the meal degenerated again to watery stew.

At Rose Grove we were still physically comfortable. As well as the deep freeze we could run a couple of electric fires from the generator, and the heat they gave was topped up by kerosine stoves in the hall and on the landing. But psychologically the atmosphere was bad. Ellen was still pale and lethargic and reluctant to eat; and Mother worried about her at the same time as resenting Mr. Gerald. Mr. Gerald had been pleasant to both Mother and Father while he was a wanted guest, and if he'd been able to extend his visit without resorting to hints of blackmail, no doubt he'd have been pleasant to both of them still. As it was, he kept up an appearance of cordiality toward Father, but didn't make much effort to ingratiate himself with Mother. It would have been no use if he had. She detested him.

Actually, it seemed to me that Mr. Gerald was pushing his luck a bit. He had started asking for particular dishes—and they weren't austere ones, either—and ordering Mother around as if she were a servant. Mother was used to getting this treatment from Father, but had always regarded it as his right. She found it hard to take from Mr. Gerald.

It was a Monday teatime when Nessie breezed into the house with Terry and the dog Peggy. Ellen, suddenly brightening, flung herself at Nessie. Peggy flung herself at everybody else. There was noise and excitement where a minute ago there had been silence and gloom. Father was still at the shop, and Mr. Gerald was ensconced in lone splendor in the sitting room, which the rest of us had ceased to use.

When Mother had taken her turn at embracing Nessie, she thrust her to arm's length and held her with both hands on her shoulders.

"You look well, our Nessie!" she said.

That was what I was thinking, too. Withdrawing from Father's protection didn't seem to have done Nessie any harm. Her cheeks were healthily pink, her eyes sparkled.

"Yes, you look great!" I said.

"I feel great." Then, to Ellen, "Hello, poppet. You're a pale poppet, aren't you? I wish we could do something for *you.*"

"Maybe she'd be better off with you," Mother said. The remark was made wistfully, not as a serious suggestion. But Nessie took it up at once.

"Of *course* she would. Why not?"

"But . . . no, Nessie, love, it's impossible. I don't know how Terry's mother manages as it is."

"She's one of nature's managers," said Nessie. "And I don't know that it's impossible. Terry, is it impossible for Ellen to come and live with us?"

"Nothing's impossible," said Terry, "except striking a match on a piece of soap. Hey, Ellen, would you like to come and live with me and Peggy?"

"*Could* I?" Ellen said, with sudden hope in her eyes.

"Don't go too fast, Terry," said Nessie. "We'd have to ask your mum first. She's taken in me and the dog already. There must be a limit, even for her."

"I keep telling you, she likes people. The more the merrier. And she knows Ellen. She likes Ellen."

"But . . . in *these* days," Mother said. "Another mouth to feed."

"I don't think that's the kind of thing that worries Mrs. Timpson," Nessie said. "If it did, she'd say so. But look, I was going to suggest that we should all go round there for a cup of tea. We can talk to her about it then."

We left a note on the kitchen table for Geoff, who was late home from school because of a club meeting. We didn't say anything to Mr. Gerald. We all just went.

It was a strange and, for our household, an extraordinarily animated little party that set off down the drive: Mother, Nessie, Terry, Ellen, and me. Something made us all link arms together, with Nessie in the middle, Ellen on one side of her and Mother on the other, Terry and me on the outside.

"The point really is," said Nessie quietly to Mother, "could you bear to part with Ellen?"

"I could bear it if it was better for *her*," Mother said. "And maybe I could do a bit to help with feeding her, same as I do with Peggy."

"Sure you could," said Terry. "Good stuff, that dog food. We all enjoy it."

It wasn't very witty, but it made everybody laugh. Arm

in arm and laughing, we spread all over the drive as we made our way from Rose Grove. I half expected Father to appear and cast a damper on us, but no. We didn't catch sight of him all the way down to Terry's.

Mrs. Timpson's tiny living room was warm, as before.

"I see you still keep the log fire going," I said to Terry.

"Keeping it going so far," Terry said. "It gets harder, mind you. Too many people after too little wood. Don't know what I'll do when the days get longer and I start running out of darkness."

"Too much of what that lad does is done in the dark," said Mrs. Timpson.

"Oh, I don't know," Terry said. "Not as much as used to be, is it, Nessie?"

"That'll do!" his mother said sharply. "Well now, this must be Nessie's mum. And here's Ellen. Hello, pet, how are you these days? Looking a bit pale since I saw you last."

"I just can't get her to eat," Mother said.

"Chance is a fine thing," said Mrs. Timpson.

"It's not that we don't *have* anything, Mrs. Timpson," said Mother. "It's just that she hasn't any appetite."

"Well, now, Ellen, pet," Mrs. Timpson said, *"you're* a funny one, aren't you? You've got food and you don't want it. There's plenty that want it and haven't got it, you know that?"

"Yes," said Ellen. "I can't help it. I just don't feel hungry."

"Not hungry?" Terry said. "I don't believe it. *'Course* you're hungry. I was always hungry at your age, and there wasn't a crisis then. Here, how about some dripping toast?"

"Dripping toast?"

"Toast with dripping on. You know what toast is, don't you? You get a nice slice of bread, and you hold it at the fire till it's just brown each side, and it's nice and crisp on the outside but just a little bit soft in the middle, and then you put lots of dripping on it, lashings of dripping, and the dripping sort of melts into the toast and goes all lovely and runny, and when you eat it you have to lick round your mouth quick, or it runs all over your chin. . . . Mmmmm. Are you *sure* you're not hungry, Ellen?"

Ellen was beginning to giggle.

"I don't know," she said.

"Just think of it, biting into that toast, all hot and yummy and absolutely *dripping* with dripping. . . . Hey, if you did feel hungry, that's exactly what we've got. Lots of bread for toasting, and lots of dripping to put on it."

"You're all just in time for tea," Mrs. Timpson said.

"Oh, we couldn't," Mother protested.

" 'Course you could," said Terry. "We got plenty, honest we have. I been doing a bit of night work."

"We have plenty for today, really we do," Mrs. Timpson said.

"And what about tomorrow?"

"Tomorrow never comes," said Terry.

"Nessie, what *does* Terry do to get bread and potatoes?" I asked her quietly.

"Oh, it's honest. It may not be strictly legal, though. The place where he works, they make kitchenware, when they can get anything to make it from. They pay the wages partly in pans and things. Then Terry cycles out to the country after dark and trades them at farms or country stores. It's a bit laborious, but it works. So long as he keeps his job, we're among the lucky ones."

We all ate dripping toast. Ellen had three slices. There was a power cut, so we sat and talked by firelight.

"It's lovely and warm here," Mother said wistfully. "Our house never *feels* warm, even when it *is*, if you know what I mean."

"It's a house without warmth," Nessie said. And then, "It'd do Ellen a world of good to stay here a bit. Would that be possible?"

"As long as she likes," Mrs. Timpson said promptly.

"Well, p'raps for a week or two," said Nessie. "How'd you like that, Ellen?"

Ellen looked first eager, then uncertain. She turned to Mother, questioningly.

"It's up to you, dear," Mother said. "If they can have you, you can stay."

But Ellen wasn't sure that she wanted to be away from Mother.

"Well, why don't you stay as well?" Mrs. Timpson asked Mother.

"Just for a little while," Nessie added hurriedly.

"But . . . you wouldn't have room?"

" 'Course there's room," said Terry. "Me and Peggy can sleep on the floor here, and we'll put Ellen in the airing cupboard—that'll be a bit of a squash, but she'll go in all right if we double her legs back . . ."

Ellen's eyes widened in alarm until she realized that Terry was teasing. Then she began giggling again. "You're a silly person," she told him. "You're the silliest person I know."

"I think," Nessie whispered to me, "that Ellen's in love with Terry. I'll have to watch it, or she'll cut me out."

"Well, that's settled, then," Terry said. "You're both

staying. Till you get tired of us. Or we get tired of you. Which do you think will happen first, Ellen?"

"I won't get tired of *you*," Ellen said.

Mother's gaze moved from Mrs. Timpson to Terry and back again. She wasn't used to such casual decisions in matters of importance like staying with people. Then I saw a wild, almost daring look come into her eyes.

"All right," she said. "If you really can manage it, if you really don't mind, yes, we'll both come. I can bring enough rations for both of us. We'll pack our bags tomorrow and come. Just for a while, of course. Not for good."

Nessie went over to Mother and put her arms round her.

"That was great, Mum," she said. "The best thing you've ever done. Now just stick to it. No turning back."

"What about Mr. Gerald?" I asked.

"Mr. Gerald," said Mother resolutely, "can either look after himself for a few days or go home. And I'd like it best if he went home."

I nearly went on to say, "What about Dad? He's in all kinds of trouble already." But then I looked at Mother, at Nessie, at Ellen, and at the Timpsons, all cheerful and happy in the firelight, ignoring the power cut. I did a little quiet weighing in the balance. And I knew on which side the balance came down.

12

"MOTHER! MOTHER!" Father's voice sounded through the house. He came into the kitchen, where Geoff and I were doing our homework on a corner of the table. "Where's your mother?" he demanded crossly. "Never here when she's wanted!"

"There's a note for you there," I said.

"A note? A note for me?"

Father picked up the envelope from the kitchen table. It was addressed simply to "Dad." He ripped it crudely open with his thumb, read it, then stared first at me and then at Geoff. "Is it a joke or something?" he asked.

"Is what a joke?"

"This." He passed the note across. All it said was, "Have gone away for a few days with Ellen, to give her a break. May."

"She can't have," he said. "She *can't* have. Not without telling me."

"Looks as if she has," I said. "She's not in the house."

Father strode to the door. I thought for a moment that he was going to search the house, unable to accept that Mother could actually have gone. But he came back and sat down.

"Where is she?" he demanded.

I looked across the table at Geoff. "Do *you* know where she is?" I asked.

"No," said Geoff. "She didn't say anything to me about it."

I hadn't told Geoff anything. I thought a reaction of honest bafflement from him would help to cover Mother's tracks.

"So neither of you know anything about it?" Father asked.

"No," said Geoff again. I lied without words by shaking my head.

"Not telling me where she's gone!" Father said. "That's deceitful. As bad as going without asking. She knew I wouldn't have stood for it. She knew!"

"I suppose that's why she didn't tell you," I said.

"It's not good enough, after all these years. I wonder where she'd go. There's her cousin Emily's in Birmingham, but I don't know how she'd get there, with no trains running. And there's that Mrs. Armitage she used to visit, near to where we lived before. They were always a bit too close for my liking. . . . The Armitages are on the telephone. I'll ring them."

He went to the phone, but was back within a minute.

"Not there," he said. "They could be hiding her, but I don't think so. I just asked if she was with them and they said 'no,' quite innocent."

He looked across at me speculatively.

"That young chap of Nessie's," he said. "I suppose *he* wouldn't have anything to do with it?"

"I don't see why he should," I said.

"Where does he live?"

"Can you remember, Geoff?" I asked.

"Never knew," said Geoff. "I haven't been there." That was true. And Geoff went on, "Anyway, Dad, she says it's only for a few days. She'll be back. I guess we can manage."

"What surprises me is that she could go at all," Father said, in a subdued tone. "If she can do that, she might do anything."

He sat silently then for what seemed a long time. Neither Geoff nor I said anything, but we didn't take up our homework again, either. I became aware of the ticking of the kitchen clock. Father was rolling and unrolling a handkerchief, not noticing what he was doing.

"You know, she mightn't come back at all," he said at last.

"May!" That was Mr. Gerald, shouting from the sitting room. "May!" He appeared in the kitchen doorway. "Where is she? MAY!"

"It's no good making all that noise," Father said coldly. "She isn't here."

"Oh. And where is she?" Mr. Gerald seemed almost as affronted as Father by the thought that Mother wasn't there awaiting his beck and call.

"She's gone away for a few days, to give Ellen a break. The child's not been well."

"Why didn't she tell me she was going?"

"She doesn't have to tell you everything," Father said.

"I expect to be looked after," Mr. Gerald said, "and made reasonably comfortable. As a guest."

"You mean you expect to be looked after, or else?"

"That's a crude way of putting it, Norman."

"That's what it amounts to." Father's tone was flat and

weary, and he didn't sound as if he cared so much as before. "Now listen, Gerald. I've been thinking about this. You can give me away, it's true. But if you do, it's the end of your stay here, isn't it? So let's get down to brass tacks. I have to treat you well enough for it to be better worth your while to stay than to go. That's all. You've been getting away with too much. Well, while May's away you won't have it quite so easy. You'll have to make do with the same as us, and be thankful for it."

Mr. Gerald didn't like the sound of that. His eyes narrowed. But he didn't make any retort. He withdrew in the direction of the sitting room.

"Well, you two lads," Father said, "I suppose we'll have to see what we can do about some supper. One way and another, we have our backs to the wall, haven't we? But I know I can rely on you." He smiled wintrily. "I know *you* won't let me down, any more than I'd let you down. Barry and Geoff, I want to tell you now, I'm proud of you, I trust you, I know you're loyal."

Solemnly he shook hands with us.

"A man and his sons," he said, "are a strong unit. I might almost say, invincible."

Father went in search of ingredients from which to put together a meal. None of us had learned to cook; Mother had looked after us too well, and Father had always regarded cooking as woman's work. We concocted a rudimentary supper as best we could. When it was ready I took Mr. Gerald's share to him on a tray. He looked at it with distaste.

"Sausages and baked beans?" he said. "What kind of a meal do you call that?"

He ate it, all the same. I had just collected the tray, and

Father and I were washing dishes, when the front door-bell rang. Geoff went to answer it, then put his head round the kitchen door and said, "It's Mr. Holloway to see you." And into the room, without waiting to be asked, came Vince Holloway, Mel's father.

Father didn't pretend to be pleased to see him. It was a visit we had all been half expecting since the evening when Geoff and I caught Mel hanging around our house.

"Hello, Norman," Vince Holloway said.

"Good evening, Mr. Holloway," Father replied in a hard, abrupt voice, with considerable emphasis on the "Mister."

"Evening," said Vince, nodding to me.

"My son, Barry," Father said. "You know him?"

"I didn't before. I do now."

"And this is Geoff."

Another nod for Geoff.

Vince Holloway was a dark, beaky-nosed, thick-eyebrowed, handsome man. A handsome *young* man, you'd probably have said at first sight, because his hair was styled and his clothes cut in the latest fashion, and he was trim around the midriff. But if you looked more closely into his face you'd see that he was at least thirty-five and more probably forty.

"You two lads can go," he said shortly. "It's your dad I want to talk to."

"Half a minute!" said Father, nettled. "Who says they can go? This is *my* house. *I'll* say whether my own sons can stay or not."

"All right, Norman, all right," said Vince. "It's only that this is a private matter. A very confidential one. I don't think you'll want it scattered to the four winds."

"My sons are in my confidence completely," Father told him. "Anything you have to say can be said in front of them."

"So be it, then. Let them stay," Vince said. "But remember it's your own decision. And I shan't mince what I have to say."

"Very well. Get on with it," said Father. I could see that Vince was the kind of man for whom he'd feel an almost instinctive dislike: flashily dressed (to his mind), sharp, flamboyant, quick-talking.

"All right, Norman. I'll come straight to the point. I have reason to think, Norman, old man, that if everybody knew all about everybody else, you'd be in trouble."

Considering that this was the second blow he'd suffered in one evening, Father took it remarkably calmly.

"I don't know what you're talking about," he said. "Explain."

"Come off it, Norman," said Vince. "You know damn well what I mean. I said I wouldn't mince words, and I won't. I know you've got a basement packed with stuff you shouldn't have. You're a hoarder, Norman. The new dirty word. A phone call to the police and it'd be three years in the nick for you, if you weren't lynched before you got there."

I had to hand it to Father. I had never known he had the slightest acting ability. But he put up a convincing performance as a man against whom a monstrous allegation had been made.

"I'll thank you to take that back, *Mister* Holloway," he said. "And then to remove yourself from my premises at once. Or perhaps you'd rather wait for me to call the police to remove you. Then you'd see whether I'm afraid to have them here."

For a moment I thought it would work. But it didn't. Vince Holloway was sure enough of himself to be able to call that bluff. He laughed derisively in Father's face, then sat down uninvited.

"Go on, then," he said. "Prove it. Call them. I'm not leaving here until I've finished."

"Shall we throw him out, Dad?" Geoff suggested.

Vince laughed again, and Father hushed Geoff with a gesture. Father stood there silent with a dishcloth in his hand, his face showing that for the moment he was defeated. Vince took a miniature cigar out of a silver case, lit it, and blew out smoke in a leisurely way. I had the impression that he was enjoying himself.

"I want you to understand me, Norman," he said. "I'm not blaming you, I'm not threatening you, nothing of that sort. I admire you. You're a man who showed foresight. That's a quality I like, foresight. And now you're showing backbone. That's another quality I like, backbone."

Father, lips pressed together, said nothing.

"All right," Vince said, "so you're breaking the regulations, you're risking a sentence. Up to three years' imprisonment and an unlimited fine. They were clever, making it an unlimited fine. If they'd fixed a sum, it would have been out of date within a week. So there you are. Prison, a fine, and, of course, confiscation of the stuff. It's pretty fierce, Norman."

"I still don't know what you're talking about," Father said.

"You're a stubborn man as well as everything else," said Vince admiringly. "Well, I don't blame you. Don't admit anything, that's a good principle. I approve of that.

All right, so you're not admitting anything and I'm just talking to myself, that's understood. Now the point is, Norman—you see, I'm on your side all the way, if you did but know it—the law only tells you what's legal, it doesn't tell you what's honest. To think ahead, well, there's nothing wrong about that, is there? To look after your family, there's nothing wrong with that, either. You're an honest family man who looks after his own. That's what you are, Norman, and I like you for it.

"Now, as for me, I'm a businessman. And it seems to me, too, that nowadays there's no need to feel too much bound by the letter of the law. So long as I'm honest, that's all I care about. And it's perfectly honest to buy things when they're cheap and sell them when they're dear. That's business. And it seems to me, Norman, from the picture I've built up—which I think is quite an accurate picture; I've had a good pair of eyes working for me—it seems to me that an astute person, a businessman, a person like me, could cash in very nicely on what you've built up."

Father looked at his watch.

"I suppose what you're saying means something to you," he said. "It doesn't mean anything to me. And I have other things to do besides listening to you."

"Very good, Norman, very good. You're keeping up your performance nicely. I approve of that. Well, now, what you're saying to yourself—although being a canny person you're not saying it to me—what you're saying to yourself is, you're not going to sell your stock, because you'd only get worthless money for it, wastepaper. You'd rather keep it for your family, that's what you're saying to yourself. Quite right, too, Norman. Put your own family first. A good principle. I approve of that. But now, what I'm saying to you is that half of what you have would be ample for your needs. Because you've overprovided, haven't you? You've enough for years. The crisis won't go on for years. Somebody has to do something about it before long. Not that I'm criticizing you for overproviding. You know what you're about, Norman. It could even be that it occurred to you that you could make a profit as well as look after yourself and yours. That would be just like a man with forethought. That would be just like you."

Vince paused, and drew on the tiny cigar.

"But of course you've said to yourself, how can you clear a profit? Not by selling for paper money; no, we've ruled that out. Not by barter; no, not for the amount of stuff you have. You're not short of anything much that might be bartered, anyway. You've always been a thrifty householder. And barter's dangerous. Every person you do a deal with could be the one who gives you away. That's right, isn't it, Norman? You've thought of that, haven't you? Of course you have. And here you are, a man with intelligence and forethought, but you're at a loss. You don't know how to realize the profit you might be making."

"I'm not out for profit," said Father.

"O—ho! O—ho!" Vince roared with laughter. "So I'm not talking to myself after all! You were off your guard then, weren't you? Never mind, I'll pretend I didn't hear. You're still admitting nothing, eh? Cautious fellow you are, Norman. I approve of that. Have a cigarlet."

"I don't smoke."

"No, of course, you wouldn't, would you? You

wouldn't send your substance up in smoke. Well now, Norman, keep on listening carefully. I'm coming to the really interesting part. There's a way in which a man in your happy position could cash in. What would you say to payment in Swiss francs, eh? Swiss francs. As good as gold, any day. You see, I'm acquainted with certain channels not known to every Tom, Dick, and Harry. And you have the good luck to be acquainted with *me*. Imagine some of your surplus being translated into Swiss francs. And in a Swiss bank account if you liked. Pounds and dollars go down and down, but the dear old Swiss franc rides high, whatever happens."

"And what cut do you get?" demanded Father, giving up the pretense that he didn't know what the conversation was about.

"Cut? Come now, Norman, when I'm dealing on behalf of an old friend I don't take a cut. That wouldn't be friendly, would it? No, I simply buy from you outright in Swiss money, cash down. Then I sell to my own outlet. I get a little more, of course, just a little, to cover my trouble. But I don't aim to make a profit. Not out of my friends, anyway."

"You can keep that idea!" Father said. "I'm having nothing to do with black market transactions." His tone was disapproving, and I was sure he was sincere.

"But Norman, you can't be serious, turning that down. A lifetime's opportunity to make some real profit and salt it safely away. Come what may, you're all right in Swiss francs."

"Listen, Holloway!" Father said. "If—just if; this is pure supposition—if I had my whole basement packed with food, I'd still keep it for my own family. Maybe you're right, maybe the crisis won't go on forever. But maybe it will go on for a lot longer than people think. I expected the worst, and it came. I'm still prepared for the worst. Perhaps the reality won't be as bad as the prospect of it. But I'll tell you this: however much I had, I wouldn't trade a teaspoonful away."

"There, there, Norman. Don't get hot under the collar. Would you like a day to think about it?"

"I don't need to think about it," Father said. "I've told you, on the assumption that I had anything anyway, the answer would be no. A firm, absolute, final no."

At last Vince gave himself a rest from talking. He drew thoughtfully two or three times on his cigarlet, looking at Father with narrowed eyes. Then he said, "I'm not taking no for an answer, Norman. Not right away. In your own interest, I don't think it's a wise answer to give."

"Are you threatening me?" Father asked.

"I'm not threatening to report you. That's not my style. Keep the police out of things, I always say. Don't worry, Norman, if the police arrive it won't be me that's put them up to it. I don't approve of that. Your problem could be quite different. Has it struck you, old man, that there's nobody you can call on for protection?"

Father didn't say anything to that.

"Just think about it," Vince went on. "Suppose a strong-arm gang came along here. Suppose they beat you up and cleaned you out of everything. Not just your surplus, the whole damned lot. And gave you nothing for it. No Swiss francs, nothing but a thick head and some cuts and bruises—and that's if you were lucky. What would you do about it, Norman? What *could* you do about it? Ever asked yourself that?"

Vince looked around for an ashtray, didn't see one,

and stubbed out his cigarlet on a plate. Then he sat back and looked at Father with an air of triumphant interrogation. There was a brief silence. Then, "Have you finished, Holloway?" Father asked in a level tone.

"*I've* finished," Vince said. "I wonder if *you've* finished, Norman. Or if you might still think better of what you've said. I'll give you a day or two, just in case."

"I admit nothing," Father said. "I accept nothing. I agree to nothing."

"If you're not careful," said Vince, "you'll *have* nothing. All right, Norman, I'll see myself out. If you have any further thoughts on this matter, give me a ring. But don't leave it too long, that's my advice."

"*I'll* see you out," said Father.

Vince laughed. "Don't worry," he said. "I'm going straight to the front door and away. I don't have to see anything, Norman. I know all I need to know."

It was Mr. Gerald, usually, who drank the brandy. Father, though not a strict teetotaler, was abstemious and rarely drank. But when Vince Holloway had gone he fetched a bottle, poured himself a generous amount, downed it rather quickly, and poured some more.

"Well," he said, "the vultures gather." His voice was weary.

That wasn't like Father at all. He had always seemed supremely confident. But just for the moment he didn't look like a man who had waited years for a challenge and was meeting it happily now it had come. He looked pale, determined but desperate. And above all he looked exhausted. His face, which never had much color, was almost gray.

I had been out of sympathy with him for months; had

indeed never really been in sympathy with him since I was old enough to have ideas of my own. But I felt sorry for him now.

"I *thought* Mel was spying," I said. "But I didn't think he'd actually seen anything he shouldn't."

"He's probably been here other times," Father said. "Before the night you caught him, or even since. We've not kept watch all the time. Anyway, it doesn't really matter how it happened. The information reached Vince Holloway, that's all that counts. He wasn't guessing. He knew."

"What was he driving at, in the end?"

"I can't be sure. That *may* have been bluff. There's no telling. But he's right, of course, in saying that if there was a break-in I couldn't do anything about it. Except of course defend myself."

Father paused, then said in a surprised tone of voice, "It's a funny thing, you know, but I quite miss having your mother around. It's because I'm used to her, I suppose. I'm doing all this for the whole family really, all six of us. It gives me an odd feeling, being down to three, as we are tonight. It's as if we'd dwindled."

"Well, we *have* dwindled," I said.

Father seemed to brace himself. A bit of the old snap returned to his voice.

"They'll be back," he said. "They'll still need my protection. And come what may, I'll still be here and able to give it them."

13

CLIFF HAD JUMPED AT THE IDEA of changing his lodgings. He'd given a week's notice at his former place at once, and was already installed in Wendy's house. This meant he was much nearer to Rose Grove than he'd been before, and he'd already suggested that I should go and visit him. The evening after the encounter with Vince Holloway I decided to take him at his word. A remark of Father's about Geoff and myself was echoing in my mind and troubling my conscience. "I'm proud of you," he'd said. "I trust you, I know you're loyal." There was no doubt about Geoff's loyalty, which was simple and unquestioning. It was myself I was doubtful about.

In a way I felt more loyal to Father than I had done a few weeks ago. There was something heroic about his stand, however wrong he might be. But did loyalty mean I had to support him in whatever he saw fit to do? Or ought I to do what I thought best for him, whether it was what he wanted or not? That was a hard question. And after Vince's reminder that there was nobody Father could call on for protection, I sensed that events were moving toward a crisis. Cliff was the only person I felt I could consult.

Wendy opened the door to me, and smiled. I realized she was glad to see me, which was pleasing.

"Hey," I said, "you look better than when I saw you last."

"I *am* better. I'm not so worried, I suppose. It's all because of Cliff. He's so kind, and he's so reliable, and he knows how to deal with things, and he understands. And he's got a job, he has wages that go up, not a pension that doesn't. And I'm going to school part of the time, because Cliff does some of the queuing."

"And your mother?"

"Oh, she's better, too. She really, truly is. Of course, she's always had ups and downs, and she was due for an upturn, but if it hadn't been for this it might never have come. Barry, I'm ever so grateful to you for bringing us Cliff. It's changed everything."

"Actually, it's Cliff I'd like to see, if he's in. It's something urgent."

"Oh. Yes, he's in," she said. I could just detect a shade of disappointment in her voice. "Yes, he's in his room. And Stuart Hazell's with him. It's upstairs and to the left."

Cliff and Stuart were talking about Share Alike when I joined them. Neither seemed very happy about it. And there was a slight edge to the conversation.

"You see, Stuart," Cliff was saying, "it's just as I always thought. Once you start on direct action, there's no logical stopping point. You finish up with hotheads like Jim Alsop calling the tune, and innocent people like Fred Birkett getting their heads split open. Fred could have been killed, you realize that?"

"You're saying 'I told you so,' aren't you?" said Stuart.

"Well, all right, if you like. But I don't want to rub it in, there's no point in that."

"No, you're not rubbing it in, you're just emphasizing that Uncle Cliff was right all along, and if only we'd listened to all his good advice . . ."

"Oh, come off it, Stuart. Never mind who was right. The fact is that Jim Alsop and the people who think like him have got the bit between their teeth. And the result is all this violence and people getting hurt, and no real redistribution at all—just a few looters who happen to be on the spot grabbing some stuff. And Share Alike getting a bad name."

"Jim Alsop's mob isn't Share Alike at all. They've broken away. They call themselves Share Now."

"And do you think the public understands the difference?"

"Frankly, no," said Stuart ruefully. "What's more, a lot of rowdies seem to be joining Share Now, and a lot of people who are just out for what they can get. You're quite right, it isn't helping us at all."

"Meanwhile," said Cliff, "the government are happy because all this creates a diversion and fills the news bulletins. And the real aims of Share Alike don't make any progress."

"All right, Cliff, that sums it up. Now tell me what to do."

"Well, it's your movement, Stuart, not mine. I'm not a member."

"You're so moderate you aren't even there," said Stuart. "If you punctured a vein, the stuff that'd come out of you would be pure milk-and-water. Listen, Cliff, the trouble is that the Alsop mob are providing all the action.

Every time there's a successful raid it's one up to them. The moderates aren't showing results. A lot of people in the movement think the lesson's all too obvious. It'll take a moderate success or two to change their minds, and there's no sign of any such thing. . . . Hello, Barry. I'm sorry you're not getting a word in edgewise. What can we do for you?"

"Well," I said, "really, I came to have a word with Cliff."

"You mean you want me out of the way?"

"Not that, exactly, but . . . can I talk to both of you in confidence? Absolute confidence?"

"It's as secret as that, eh, Barry?" said Cliff. "I wonder if it really is. If it's about your dad, it may not be."

"How do you know it's about my dad?"

"Just a hunch."

"Well, then, do you both promise not to pass anything on to anybody?"

"I'll promise not to pass on anything I didn't know already," said Cliff.

"That's fair enough," I said, and looked questioningly at Stuart.

"All right, go on," he said. "I'll buy it on the same terms."

I began by telling them about Father's hoards. But before I'd got far I noticed that they were giving each other meaningful looks. I interrupted myself.

"Have you heard something about this already?" I asked, alarmed.

"Frankly, yes," said Cliff.

"Where from?"

"Rumor, that's all. I was rather hoping it was *only* rumor. There are plenty of those around, of course, and I don't like them, because they're not all justified, by any means. Some of them come from jealousy or malice or vague suspicion, or from people putting two and two together and making five."

"And what happens when these rumors get around?"

"You can guess, can't you? As likely as not, sooner or later there's a raid. And if the rumors were wrong, it doesn't necessarily help the people who are raided. They can still get injured. And sometimes looters are so furious at not finding anything that they start wrecking a place up, just out of sheer vandalism."

"Ugh!" I said, and pulled a face.

"Anyway, is that all you have to tell us, Barry?"

"Well, no," I said, and I told them about Mr. Gerald's blackmail and the visit from Vince Holloway and the departures of Nessie and Mother and Ellen. And when I'd finished, Cliff whistled.

"Well," he said, "I had a feeling your father was up against it. He's been looking as if he had the cares of the world on his shoulders. I thought it might be because there was something in the rumors. But I didn't realize it was like that."

"I feel dreadful telling anybody. Especially you, in a way, Cliff, seeing you work with Dad. But I just don't know what to do for the best."

"The best for *whom*?" Stuart asked.

"I'm thinking of the best for him and us just now," I said. "As it is, he's running the risk of being raided, or else being reported to the police and sent to prison. And in either case he might get beaten up into the bargain. Or if he doesn't get raided or reported, he might crack up under the strain. The whole thing's got me worried."

"I look at it less narrowly," Stuart said. "I look at the public interest, as well as yours and your father's."

"Don't be pompous, Stuart," said Cliff. "Barry, let's get this straight. Are you suggesting that your dad would be better off if he could get rid of all this stuff? If so, what about the rest of you? At present you're eating while millions of people are hungry. Are you prepared to give that up?"

"It looks as if before long we won't have any choice," I said. "In any case, I think I'd be happier if we just took our chance like everybody else. There'll still be plenty who are worse off than us. After all, Dad's in work and we're all healthy."

"A very noble attitude," said Stuart.

"Don't be pompous *or* sarcastic, Stuart," said Cliff. "Now listen, Barry, if that's what you really think, it seems to me that your interest and the public interest are the same. What if your dad turned it all over to Share Alike? How would that be? You see, Stuart? Mr. Mortimer's problems solved and a big success for Share Alike, all at one go."

"O—ho!" said Stuart. He stopped and thought about that. Then he grinned. "Yes, you're right. One up to Uncle Cliff."

"If, of course, Mr. Mortimer will cooperate. And that's a big 'if.' Do you think he'll cooperate, Barry?"

"No," I said. "I don't. Dad's been obsessed with this for months. He won't throw it up just because somebody asks him to. It's his life now."

"Having worked with him for nearly two years," Cliff said, "I know he doesn't give way easily. Still, it's worth trying. Why don't I go round and talk to him?"

"It might be as much as your job's worth," Stuart said.

"Mr. Mortimer can't sack me. Only the area manager can do that. And he'd have to have good reasons. No, that doesn't worry me at all. But I'm a bit afraid that Mr. Mortimer may think Barry spilled the beans to me."

"Let me come with you," Stuart said. "And we'll tell him about the rumors but we won't tell him about Barry. I must just cycle down to the Share Alike office to pick something up, Cliff, but I'll be back in a few minutes."

"That's fine," Cliff said. "I'll impress on Mr. M. that these rumors are going around and he's taking a big risk. I'll say we don't want him to be raided and perhaps have his head split open like Fred Birkett. Barry, I think you'd better go home now. Stuart and I will come round later this evening, and of course we won't mention that we've seen you. All right?"

"All right," I said. "I wish you luck."

I was halfway up our drive when I heard a car engine start, up by the house. Then lights came on, and a few seconds later a car was heading down the drive toward me, fairly fast. I had to jump back to get out of its way. Having passed me, the car cut out an unnecessary bend in the drive by going straight across the lawn. In another two or three seconds it was out through the gate, and I heard it accelerating along the road outside until it was out of earshot.

It was all rather sudden, and the car had actually gone before I realized that it was Mr. Gerald's dark blue

Wolseley. I continued up the drive. In the front doorway was Father, staring out into the darkness.

"Where's *he* gone?" he said when he saw me.

"Who? Mr. Gerald? That was his car going down the drive."

"I know. But what's up? I saw the car standing on the gravel and him stowing something inside it. But when I spoke to him he didn't answer. Just finished whatever he was doing, then got into the driver's seat and drove away, quick. I wonder what he's up to. He doesn't usually go out in the evening."

"He may have gone to the Red Barn," I said, naming the out-of-town hotel which a lot of business people patronized. "Or—do you think there's any hope that he's gone home? Left us?"

"I wish I thought so, Barry," my father said. "But let's have a look in his room."

And when we looked into Mr. Gerald's room it was plain that he had indeed gone. Only a week or two ago he had seemed to be settling in for a long stay. Now all his personal things had disappeared; nothing was left but the bare basic furnishings of the room.

Father and I looked at each other, and Father expressed what we both felt.

"Thank God!" he said.

We had of course resented Mr. Gerald since it became obvious that he was staying on as an unwanted guest. Oddly, this resentment seemed to have been returned; it was as though Mr. Gerald liked to be admired and felt his hosts had no business not to want him. He had been rude to Mother, and I had suspected several times that there was malice beneath his surface politeness to Father.

Since Mother and Ellen had left, he'd been awkward and uncertain-tempered with all of us. The meals we'd had since then had been very simple and bachelor-style, drawing heavily on such standbys as meatballs and canned spaghetti. It was adequate nourishment, but it wasn't the kind of cuisine that appealed to Mr. Gerald. And Father had been unable to give any satisfactory reply to his repeated questions about when Mother was going to return.

Now the first smile I'd seen there for days appeared on Father's face.

"Strikes me," he said, "that what your mother did was the one way of getting rid of him."

"Perhaps that's why she did it," I suggested—not that I thought for a moment that it was.

"No, no, she hasn't the brains," Father said at once. "But if she *had* had brains, she couldn't have done better."

We went down to the hall. There Geoff met us, coming from the kitchen.

"This house smells like a distillery," he said. "What's happened?"

There was indeed a smell of spirits. Along the passage that led from the hall to the back of the house it grew stronger. And there we found the cause of it: a broken whisky bottle, and whisky soaking into the carpet.

"Who did that?" Father said. "Criminal waste of good liquor."

Then the thought came simultaneously to all of us. Father positively ran to the washroom where the cellar key was kept. It wasn't there. He ran down the steps, with both of us following. The door at the bottom was open.

199

And in places the usual immaculate neatness of the racks had been disturbed.

"The . . . !" I was sure I heard Father use an uncharacteristically rude word. He darted forward, checking what had gone. Then he used the rude word again.

"He's taken two dozen bottles each of whisky and brandy," he said. "Most of the stuff I laid in to use for swapping rather than for ourselves. *And* he's taken some cans, but only the most expensive things. Either he spent a long time choosing or he knew exactly where the things he wanted were."

"I bet he knew," said Geoff.

"I never saw him come anywhere near this part of the house," Father said.

"Nor did I," I said. "But somehow I can imagine, can't you?"

And when we put our minds to it, we all could. Those sharp, aware looks of Mr. Gerald's went with the kind of person who would know precisely what was going on, especially if it might be to his advantage.

"I can just *see* him pussyfooting around," Geoff said.

"Oh, well," I said, "it looks as if he's gone for good. Let's hope so, anyway. If he has, it's worth it."

"Yes, I reckon it's worth it," Father agreed. He sighed, all the same, at the thought of all those bottles of brandy and whisky, to say nothing of his cherished cans. Then he moved forward almost automatically to restore order in the basement.

"You two lads could go and sweep up the pieces of that bottle," he said.

As we reached the top of the cellar steps the telephone rang. Geoff answered it and called me over. It was Stuart.

"Barry!" he said. "I'm at the Share Alike office. And listen, I've just been told there was a phone call twenty minutes ago giving a tipoff about your father's stocks."

"Well, that wasn't news to you, was it?" I said, trying to make my voice sound casual, though my heart was thumping. "Do you know who rang?"

"No. It was anonymous. They always are. But I'm told it was somebody with a plummy voice and an almost-a-gentleman accent."

"I know who *that* would be," I said grimly.

"Said he had the public interest at heart. But Bill Lightner, who took the call, says he thought it was malicious. You can usually tell. Anyway, Bill told him we were a law-abiding organization, not to be confused with Share Now. And the caller didn't sound too pleased. Said he knew who to speak to next. So my guess is that Jim Alsop or somebody in his outfit probably knows all about your dad by now. And I must say I have a feeling Bill was wrong to choke this person off. If anybody's going to get your dad's stuff, it should be Share Alike."

"I suppose you and Cliff will still be coming round tonight, Stuart?" I asked.

"Oh, yes. You bet we will. This makes it all the more urgent. We may not have much time."

"It's those two pals of yours," Geoff said. He sounded slightly disgruntled. "I've just let them in. And Dad's taken them into the sitting room and switched off the television. So I have to do without the football."

"Stuart says the government are keeping football going because it's the opium of the masses," I told him.

"Stuart? Isn't he one of them?"

"Yes."

"Then I can't say that makes me any fonder of him."

Geoff showed signs of withdrawing to his own room. But I was hoping that Father would call us in for consultation.

"Have a game of chess," I said. That was an invitation that Geoff was always ready to accept. I was the better player but he was keener. Tonight I wasn't concentrating; I expected Father's summons any minute, and became dismayed as the minutes went by without it. Meanwhile Geoff steadily built up a strong position. After half an hour he was a knight to the good and had a powerful attack. When Father put his head round the door and asked us both to step into the sitting room I was relieved but Geoff looked irritated.

"All right, you've won," I said, and we followed Father. Cliff and Stuart were there, looking dogged but uncomfortable.

"Now, lads," Father said, turning to us, "Clifford and his young friend are the latest people to come here telling us they believe we have what the government says we shouldn't have. *How* they know they haven't said, but I'm getting used to that. Of course, I don't admit anything of the kind. But Clifford here has a suggestion to make, and I want you two to hear it. A lesser man than I might think it an impertinence, coming from one who's his assistant, and moreover under some obligation. But that's not my way. I'm always willing to listen, it's a principle of mine, and I'd like you two to listen as well. You see, Clifford, my sons are in my confidence. We're a unit, we stand together. So come on now, let's have it. Speak up."

"Well, as I've told you, Mr. Mortimer," Cliff began, in a mild, thoughtful tone, "it seems to me that anyone who is keeping illicit food stocks is running a big risk and ought to get rid of them in his own interest. The time for handing them in without penalty has gone. I don't think the government *want* to forgo penalties any more. They want to punish hoarders with as much publicity as possible. But I can see a solution. You've heard of Share Alike, Mr. Mortimer?"

"I've heard of it."

"It distributes what supplies it can find, as fairly as it can, to those who need them most. Stuart here is active in Share Alike. Stuart could arrange for a van to call here one night very soon—and the sooner the better; tomorrow, perhaps—to collect these supplies and take care of them. Share Alike would see that they went where they could do most good. And we can guarantee that no word would ever be said about where they came from."

He paused. Father didn't say anything.

"It would be a great load off your mind, Mr. Mortimer," Cliff added. "And perhaps a load off your conscience."

Cliff had spoken well, but with these last words he went wrong. Father bristled at once.

"My conscience?" he said. "I'd have you know, Clifford Trent, that my conscience is clear. As it always has been and always will be."

"Mr. Mortimer," Cliff said, "I haven't asked you to admit anything, but I'd rather you didn't profess indignation."

I frowned. Cliff had put a foot wrong again. Father's fists were clenched to his sides, and I could feel the tension rising. But Father kept control of himself. Eventually he said, "Clifford, I will put myself in your hands.

Yes, I do have the stocks you mention, and if you denounced me I should be sent to prison. And I dare say you would get my job. But I will not allow you—" and now his voice began to rise—"I will not *allow* you to suggest that I am not sincere or that I accept any kind of guilt whatever. Have you ever known me be insincere, Clifford? Have you?"

"No, Mr. Mortimer."

"No, I should think not."

"But when there are millions without enough to eat, Mr. Mortimer, do you really think your actions justified?"

"I do," said Father. "I do. A man's first duty is to his own." His words were firm, but his voice was beginning to sound a little ragged at the edges. "Whatever happens, no harm will come to my family while I can prevent it. I don't know any higher principle than that."

"And you'd still feel that way," Cliff asked, "if there were people at your door really, literally, starving?"

"Which there are," Stuart interposed, "except that they're not at your door, they're behind their own doors, where you can't see them."

"All right, Stuart, that'll do," said Cliff. He turned to Father again, putting on the pressure. "Would you, Mr. Mortimer? Would you turn the starving away?"

Father stood up. He unclenched his fists. "Clifford," he declared, his voice vibrant, "I would leave everyone in the world to die before I would stop protecting my own."

That was the moment at which I realized that, for all our failure to communicate with each other, I loved him. It was also the moment at which I realized I couldn't go along with him anymore. I knew now that I would desert.

"Very well, Mr. Mortimer," Cliff said quietly. "I'm not going to give you away. I'm not an informer. You must do as you think right. I hope no harm comes to any of you."

"You're leaving it at that, Cliff?" said Stuart.

"Yes."

"You've no business to." He turned toward Father, full of indignation. "You just wait and see!" he said. "If you get beaten up it'll serve you right!"

"Are you threatening me, young man?" Father asked.

"No, he's not," said Cliff. "He feels strongly, that's all. Good-bye, Mr. Mortimer."

"Good-bye, Clifford."

Father showed them out. Then he came back into the room.

"I didn't take to Clifford's friend at all," he said. "What's his name? Stuart something?"

"Stuart Hazell. He's all right. He means well," I said. "The man to watch out for is Jim Alsop."

"I know about Alsop. He's a menace, a real extremist. I saw him on the news again the other night. *He* doesn't come into this, surely?"

"He might," I said. "He's been organizing a lot of raiding parties. If he heard about us . . ."

"My God!" said Father. "I'm beset by rogues, aren't I? And Clifford, of all people, mixed up with them."

"Cliff's not a rogue," I said. "Nor is Stuart."

"All right, I agree, Clifford isn't. I'm not so sure about

the other one, though." Father sat down. There was a long silence. Then he said, "Well, lads, we're on our own now."

"You can count on *me*, Dad," said Geoff.

"Good for you, Geoff. I knew I could."

"Though I must say," Geoff went on thoughtfully, "I'd find it hard not to help someone who was actually on the doorstep. You know what I mean?"

"Of course," Father said. "Your feelings do you credit. I wouldn't expect a lad of mine to be callous. But there are times when you can't take your natural impulses as a guide, and this is one of them. Right, Geoff?"

"I suppose so."

"As for you, Barry. . . ."

"I think there's a lot to be said for handing over to Share Alike," I said slowly.

Father looked me steadily in the eye.

"I'm not altogether surprised that you say that," he told me. "You're young and idealistic, and these do-good schemes are attractive. However, I've been in the world much longer than you have. I've considered it, and I've come to a decision. I expect you to support me. Indeed, I know you will. And in spite of your scruples, I know that when it comes to a pinch your loyalty will be as strong and solid as Geoff's, and I'm just as proud of you."

I found it hard to meet his eye. I couldn't tell him I would let him down. But I knew I would, and must.

"Tonight," Father said briskly, "I shall keep watch. I don't really think anything will happen. But I don't trust Vince Holloway and I don't trust Clifford's friend. As for that Alsop fellow, words fail me. Tomorrow we'll prepare our defenses."

Father brightened visibly as he began to plan his next moves. Although the situation looked bad, it was in his nature to be stimulated by the thought of standing fast and meeting challenges head-on.

"I'll have a nap now," he said, "and you two must wake me at midnight—or before, if you see or hear anything suspicious. If all's quiet at midnight you can go to bed. I'll have that football rattle of yours with me, Geoff, and if anything happens I'll swing it for all I'm worth and you must both come down at the double. But I think tonight's too soon for trouble, really, and it's just as well, because we're not ready for it. Tomorrow you two lads had better stay off school and help me clear the decks for action."

"Is it going to be *that* bad?" I asked.

"I hope not," Father said. "But we're in for some anxious days. If nothing happens in the next week or two, that'll probably mean that nothing's *going* to happen. In the meantime, 'be prepared' is a good motto. Now, Barry, the first thing I want you to do tomorrow morning is go and talk to Nessie. You're the closest to her. Find out if she's heard anything from Mother. And tell her that when the immediate crisis is past she can come back, and bring young what's-his-name as well. I'm prepared to accept him as family. Though that would be on the basis that they intend marriage, you understand, when things are more normal."

"I don't know what they intend," I said. "They may not intend anything."

"When I was that age," Father said, "a decent lad . . . Oh, well, there's more immediate things to worry about. Anyway, Barry, I want you to make it clear to Nessie that I haven't closed the door in her face."

"All right," I said. I didn't think for a moment that Nessie would come back, but I was glad of the chance to see her.

"Then you can come back here and give us a hand. And tomorrow night, when we're better placed to hold out, we'll start keeping watches properly. You can stay on watch from ten until one, Barry, and Geoff from four until seven in the morning. I'll take the key watch, from one till four. That's when an attack would be most likely to take us by surprise."

He looked from one of us to the other.

"I hope you realize, lads," he said, "that we may have to face a siege."

I didn't sleep much that night. I was coming to a conclusion about what I must do, and it was a painful one. As the hours went by and I turned now one way, now the other, trying a hundred postures and finding comfort in none of them, I felt more and more that before I acted I must seek Father out and make a last appeal to him. And when the darkness turned to gray, I got out of bed and crept quietly down to the sitting room.

I don't know why it startled me to find Father asleep at his post. He had had a wearying and worrying time for long enough; I'd thought before now that he was exhausted. And it was just like him to take on a long stint, convinced that he could endure when in fact he couldn't. Yet it did surprise me to see that even Father's vigilance could fail.

He was sitting in a cane-bottomed chair, turned toward the window. On the floor in front of him lay Geoff's football rattle, decked in the colors of our local team. One hand held the butt of the revolver, which lay in his lap. His head had dropped to his chest. His face was gray and stubbly, and I noticed for the first time that it was becoming lined. He looked his full fifty-two years. As I watched, he muttered something in his sleep, half started, seemed as if he might wake, then went off again.

I gazed at him for a minute or so: a lonely, darkened man; devoted, stubborn, and infinitely determined. He would not be made less dogged by the knowledge that he had slept on duty. To plead with him would be a waste of breath. He would never yield.

I went silently back to bed and slept until the alarm clock rang.

14

FRIDAY, THE EIGHTH OF MARCH. The second and last snow of
winter had been brief, but fast-falling and heavy-flaked,
with the temperature already on the rise. Now trees and
bushes were drenched and dripping, and city streets
were deep in slush. The occasional ambulance, truck, or
police or army vehicle sprayed murky liquid over the
passersby who trudged, booted, through ankle-high
filth. Bicycles—now a popular means of transport,
cherished and carefully guarded by their owners—
skidded along the treacherous trackways left by larger
vehicles. The trickle of thawing snow sounded from
drainpipes and gutters.

At the supermarket which I passed on my way to the
welfare center there was a little line of people, mostly
young to middle-aged, but nothing like the queues
there'd been as recently as the previous week. Change
came rapidly now. The inflation bubble was blowing up
to spectacular dimensions. The government had suddenly taken off the price controls, because there just
weren't the goods to go round, and ration tickets were
useless. Today you could buy a loaf of bread if you'd a
million pounds in your purse, a can of beans for two

million, a quarter pound of corned beef for just over three. Tomorrow you'd probably need a million and a half, three million and five million pounds for the same purchases. If you were in work you could just about manage it. You might be earning ten million pounds a day today. By Monday it would have gone up to fifteen. Your wife or husband would be waiting at the factory gate to grab your day's wage and spend it before the midday price rise.

But those in work were the lucky ones. The old and the unemployed outnumbered them. And all efforts to keep pensions and benefits in line with the cost of living had been abandoned. The old age pension, stuck somewhere in the thousands of pounds a week, would literally not buy a crust. There wasn't any point in lining up to draw it. The sick and the old and the out-of-work were destitute. Small shops were now admitted to be in business for barter only. People sidled furtively through the streets toward them with strange bumps under their coats. A teapot or a table lamp could be exchanged for enough food to hold off hunger for a few more hours; and if you had no tea for the pot and no electricity for the lamp, you didn't really need them. The only things you didn't sell were your blankets. When all else failed, you'd take refuge in those.

Bands of men roamed the streets, watched from the army trucks which now formed most of the traffic. In the city center, the main stores were well guarded and the streets patrolled. You could walk along the pavement with packages in your shopping basket—if you were lucky enough to have any—and nobody would assault you, though someone might well try a quick grab-and-run. Away from the city center the army and police couldn't be everywhere, and there was a fair amount of violence. Street brawls took place mainly in the daytime, often for no obvious reason, but food raids were usually carried out in darkness. I'd heard Stuart Hazell say there was a sense in which they were necessary, because the stocks in shops and private hoards were the only fat left on the body of the nation, and people must live on whatever fat there was. The question, for him, was how the fat should be distributed.

At the center this morning there was no queue, which was a surprise until I saw Mike at the side door with a placard reading SORRY, NO MEALS. He was arguing with a few old people who couldn't take the placard's word for it and were sure that if they stayed around long enough there would be something for them in the end. "We might be back in business on Monday," Mike was telling all comers. "We hope."

I had seen Nessie, as Father had asked. I hadn't thought for a moment that she would come home, with or without Terry, and I was quite right. But I'd been able to consult her and Mother on what I proposed to do, and they both agreed.

Mother was in an odd state of mind. After twenty years of marriage she found it hard to believe that she had actually done something without Father's consent—and something so drastic as leaving him, even if it was only for a short time. She worried continually about him and about how we were managing. I had no doubt she'd have come home pretty quickly if it hadn't been for Ellen. But Ellen was visibly better and happier, and that had decided Mother so far. She had to put Ellen first.

And now, before going home, I had the opportunity to see Cliff and Stuart, and to put my decision into effect. They were sitting opposite each other in the tiny office behind the center, looking glum.

"Seems like we'll have to go onto a two-day week," Cliff told me. "Supplies get less and less, and we just can't feed all our customers. It'll have to be Mondays and Thursdays now, unless things improve. There were headlines in the *Record* today about an international support operation, and relief ships being loaded on the Continent, but frankly, I'll believe in all that when I see it."

"What about the people who can't get out and just have to rely on the meals-on-wheels? Does it mean a two-meal week for them as well?" I asked.

" 'Fraid so," said Cliff.

"Quite a thought, isn't it?" said Stuart. "The last quarter of the twentieth century, and it's a two-meal week for some. And they're the lucky ones. If that's all we care about old people, why don't we just let them die?"

"Barry has his own problems," said Cliff. "Namely, his dad. That's right, isn't it, Barry? I wish we could have persuaded him to hand over. Seems to me that he can't last long."

"Is the news really going to get around?" I asked.

"I don't see how we can stop it, even if it hasn't got to Jim Alsop already."

"If you ask me," said Stuart, "Bill Lightner was wrong to choke off that informer. *Somebody's* going to get your dad's stuff before long. It ought to be Share Alike."

"Actually," I said, feeling more treacherous than ever in my life, "I agree with you. And I want Share Alike to get it as soon as possible."

Cliff and Stuart both stared at me. But I knew what I

was saying. I'd lain awake most of the night working it out.

"*I'm* not pretending it's the public interest," I said. "Not really. It's Dad I'm worrying about. He's heading for disaster."

"He certainly is," said Stuart.

"You said you could arrange for a Share Alike van to come round at night. Well, why don't you do just that?"

"You mean *we* should carry out a raid?" Stuart asked.

"No, no. Not that," Cliff said anxiously.

"Not *exactly* that," I told them. "Because they won't have to break in. They'll be *let* in."

"Oh?" said Stuart. "Who by?"

"Me," I said.

There was a long pause. My heart thumped, and I was trembling. Cliff put an arm round my shoulders.

"Barry, lad," he said. "Think. Think what you're doing. So far, Stuart and I haven't heard a word, have we, Stuart?"

"No," said Stuart unexpectedly. "It's a big decision for you to make, Barry. Hadn't you better talk about it before you take that on yourself?"

"I have thought," I said. "And I've spoken to Mother and Nessie, and they agree with me. I haven't talked to Geoff. He'll stick to Father through thick and thin. If I tell him, he'll just tell Dad and that will be an end of it. So I can't. But I've thought about what I'm doing. My God, I've thought till I'm dizzy."

"Well, if you're really sure," said Stuart, "I might as well tell you, I think you're absolutely right."

"I'm sure it's right that your dad's stuff should be

handed over," Cliff said. "I'm not so sure that you're right to go over his head. Or that Share Alike should be taking the stuff on your tipoff, so to speak."

"Your trouble, Cliff, is an outsize conscience," said Stuart.

"I suppose so," said Cliff, looking worried, as if that were an additional problem.

"Anyway, Barry, tell us how you'll do it," Stuart said.

"Well, today we're getting dug in, in readiness for an attack. And from tonight we're taking watches. I shall be doing ten until one, Dad's doing one till four, and Geoff four till seven. Dad reckons one to four's the biggest danger. He says he'll go to bed early. So it seems to me that if the Share Alike van can come at eleven, he's sure to be asleep. I'll unlock the door for you. And as long as everybody's quiet, the whole job can be done before one."

"And supposing it all comes off," Cliff asked, "what's your dad going to say to *you* when he finds out?"

"Or *do* to you?" Stuart added.

"I won't tell him what I've done," I said. "Not so much because of what he might do to me, but because it'd break his heart. I'll let him find me asleep when he comes down at one o'clock to take his watch."

"Will he believe you could have slept through it all?"

"Well, something happened that in a way is lucky. I found *him* asleep this morning. If *he* can sleep on watch, so can I."

"Yes, but I don't suppose he'd have stayed asleep while his entire stores were taken," Cliff said.

"Maybe not. Share Alike will have to be very quiet anyway, so as not to wake him or Geoff. There's quite a risk of that, after all. As for suspecting me, I don't think he will. He'll be disappointed in me, in fact he'll be furious, but he won't believe I've betrayed him."

"I don't like the sound of it," Cliff said. "Not at all."

"I was just thinking I *did* rather like the sound of it," said Stuart. "Neat, useful, solves all the problems at once. And listen, Barry, you don't have to give every last ounce away. You can still keep a few cans for emergencies. Lots of people have that, it's all right within reason."

"Here, not so fast," Cliff objected. "What's Bill Lightner going to say? He's as law-abiding as I am. He's always resisted attempts to make Share Alike militant."

"I shall tell Bill it's to be done with the consent of the householder," Stuart said. "We've done it two or three times before, when people wanted to part with their stocks quietly and not get into trouble. It won't surprise him. He'll be delighted. It's high time we had something more to distribute."

He was full of enthusiasm, eager to act.

"But listen, both of you . . ." Cliff began.

"Are you proposing to stop us, Cliff?" asked Stuart.

"No, but . . ."

"Then help me to work it out," Stuart said. "Or if you won't do that, keep quiet."

"I can't stay long," I said. "I must be getting home. Dad'll wonder what's become of me. And I don't want to do anything to make him suspicious."

I wondered at first who it was in our garden, digging in the sand heap with Geoff. It was a few seconds before I realized that it was Father wearing battle dress, brought out from some drawer or other after more than thirty years. I'd never seen him in it, except in old photographs.

On the shoulders were his two pips, for after being a sergeant through most of the Hitler war he'd been commissioned at the end of it and finished as a lieutenant. The battle dress still fitted him; Father hadn't put on weight. A webbing belt round his waist carried the holster for his gun. He had a beret on his head—not, I guessed, because it was needed, but because he'd feel improperly dressed without it.

"Well," he said, "and where have *you* been all this time?"

"I went to see Nessie, as you told me."

Father was eyeing me. "You hold yourself in a sloppy way, Barry," he said. I thought for a moment he was going to rap out a command to stand to attention, but he didn't. I shuffled uneasily. He went on, "Well, what did she say?"

"She says she's not coming back, either now or when the crisis is over."

"That girl," said Father, "has no more sense than she has morals." But I knew he wasn't really surprised. He went straight on, "Did you find anything out about Mother?"

"I don't know any more about Mother than I did before," I said truthfully.

"You've got no results, then. Is that all you've done?"

"I went to see Cliff as well. And Stuart Hazell."

"I can't see any point in talking to *them*. Did they put on the pressure again to hand over to that do-good organization?"

"As a matter of fact, they didn't. They were upset because they can't get enough supplies for the center. It'll probably go on a two-day week."

"People should remember the fable of the ants and the grasshopper," Father said. "We're the ants. Well, Barry—" and there was a brisk, almost military ring to his voice—"you seem to have spent half a morning achieving precisely nothing. Never mind. Geoff and I have been busy. We've boarded up the basement and downstairs windows already. One pane of glass broken, which isn't bad, considering. And now we're going to sandbag the windows and doors. You're fresh and we're tired. You can take a turn with the spade."

The tarpaulin had been rolled back from the sand heap. The sand was reasonably dry, though caked. I dug while Geoff or Father held a bag open; then all three of us would heave it onto a wheelbarrow and Geoff or Father would push it away toward the area steps at the side of the house. Then the sandbags had to be maneuvered down the steps and into place behind the basement windows. This was heavy work, and frequently all three of us were needed again. Father seemed tireless, and offered unending praise and encouragement. I realized that in some strange way he was enjoying himself immensely. This was his challenge. This was his element.

At midday we took a break and ate soup and thick corned beef sandwiches. Father poured beer for us to drink. "You're men today," he said. "Men! I can't treat you as children now. Not that I ever thought much of lemonade or cola or any kind of colored muck. Beer is a man's drink. In moderation, of course. Strict moderation." And considering how thirsty we were, he didn't really give us any too much.

After lunch we finished fortifying the basement. We left a few filled sandbags just inside the door at the foot of the area steps. Then we went in through the door for the last time and blocked it from within. While the door had stood open, the basement had looked no more gloomy than usual, but now it became suddenly dark. The only light—and it wasn't of any practical use—was a mosaic-like pattern thrown on the floor from an old-fashioned perforated metal ventilation grid, set into the wall at the back of the house. Father switched the light on, then examined the grid thoughtfully. It was about eighteen inches wide and twelve deep, and looked rusty.

"That *could* be a security risk," he said. "But I don't quite know how we'd block it. We can't cut off the ventilation. And it won't be easily seen, being round the back and behind those bushes. Which reminds me . . . what about the coal hole?"

With some effort we blocked the coal chute, then replaced the round metal grid that covered it. And then we had to set to work on the ground floor. Every bag of sand now had to be wheeled into the house up an inclined plank over the three steps to the front door. As the afternoon wore on, the work grew heavier and progress seemed slower. Geoff and I grew irritable, and more and more disposed to take rests. But Father remained cheerful, rallied the troops as necessary, and did the work of two. He knew exactly the moment to give us a tea break. By dusk the sandbagging was done.

Father had worried slightly about whether the house would look obviously barricaded. But it didn't. The windows had been boarded behind Mother's white net curtains, and it would have taken a close inspection to reveal anything unusual. The effect inside was much more disconcerting. Although gaps had been left so that we ourselves could look out, and the sandbags were not stacked to the very tops of the window frames, the amount of daylight coming in was reduced so sharply that the whole ground floor was in virtual darkness, and artificial light would be needed all day. This gave me a feeling of claustrophobia. Father noticed it too, and remarked that we could use the guest bedroom upstairs for sitting in during the day. Geoff, stolid in temperament and not very sensitive to such considerations, seemed unaffected.

The last item was the front door. Obviously we ourselves had to be able to get into and out of the house. Father had worked out a device for dealing with this. Horizontally across the inside of the door itself, about three feet above floor level, we screwed a stout piece of wood from an old gate. Across the floor, three feet back and parallel with it, we fixed another. Then we cut the ends of two more pieces of timber at an angle so that they could be inserted as buttresses, with their ends wedged against the other two. They were jammed tight, but could be tapped out of place with a mallet when we wanted to use the door. They would take a great deal of strain.

"You'd need twenty men with a battering ram to get through that," said Father with satisfaction when the job was done. "And now we've finished, we'll have a real slap-up feed." And we ate bacon and sausages and baked beans and canned tomatoes.

After supper, Geoff was nodding with physical exhaustion. He'd started work before I did, and hadn't stopped all day. I was in a state of acute anxiety and guilt. All day, as we worked—and Father and Geoff had worked hard, almost heroically—I had felt myself more and more to be a traitor. Yet every time I went through the arguments in my head the result was the same. Father was deceiving himself. He had to lose. The best thing for him was to get his stocks safely into the hands of Share Alike before he was sent to jail, or worse. To betray him was the only way to save him. It had to be done.

Father himself was still in an exalted mood. He brushed down his battle dress, and was pleased that it hadn't suffered much from the day's exertions. He gave himself, as a special treat, a glass of whisky. I could see him eyeing us and wondering whether in view of our new status as men he could offer it to us as well, but he must have decided that that was going too far. He poured each of us another glass of beer, though.

Then, inspired perhaps by the battle dress, the two pips on his shoulder, and the mess atmosphere induced by the drinks, he gave us some of his wartime reminiscences. We'd heard a few of them before, but others were new. Father had not in fact been in action against the enemy, so his battles had been entirely within the hierarchy of his own side. He told of seniors who had tried to treat him as a nobody and been discomfited, or who had been consistently wrong in some question of organization when he was consistently right. He told of subordinates who had tried to trick him as quartermaster, but had tried in vain, because Father knew all the tricks. He told of the commanding officer who had delayed his commission because he knew that Father would be promoted away from the unit, and Father was too valuable to him as a sergeant. If it hadn't been for this, Father said, he would undoubtedly have finished the war as a major, if not a colonel, instead of a mere lieutenant. Then no doubt the Bowlings or their successors would have treated him accordingly and given him his rightful place on the board.

At this point, bitterness began to creep into Father's voice, but he overcame it. He had always been a good man in a tight spot, he told us, and we were certainly in a tight spot now. But as he'd said before, if we could get through the next couple of weeks we'd be all right. And although the country had been let down by lazy and incompetent and ill-intentioned people, the country as a whole would also pull through. It was right that people should suffer the consequences of their failures, and it would be wrong to cushion them. In the end, the ordeal would prove to have done everybody good. The future was bright.

I had a feeling that, for the moment anyway, Father was happier than he'd been in years. There was an almost Churchillian ring to his voice.

Geoff was so sleepy that we almost had to put him to bed. And halfway through the evening, while still reminiscing, Father, too, began to yawn. Reminding me that he had to begin his watch at one in the morning, he went to bed before ten. I was in charge and on my own until one, and I didn't think either of them would wake.

However, I didn't ring Stuart until I could actually hear Father's heavy breathing through his bedroom door.

"We're all dug in," I told Stuart then. "I'm on watch now, and they're fast asleep. I've been wondering if the job could be done tonight, so it's all over. I don't think I can stand the strain for long."

"Sorry," Stuart said. "Sorry. Tomorrow night, yes. Tonight, no. I haven't the van or the people."

I was deeply disappointed.

"You realize," I said, "that if Jim Alsop or somebody of that sort has had a tipoff, we might be attacked at any time? There may be people creeping up on us this minute for all I know."

"I know," said Stuart. "If anything happens, give me a ring and we'll do what we can, which may not be much. But tomorrow night we'll definitely be there. Can you promise to let us in?"

"Yes. I'll unblock the front door for you. But we must remember to push in the ventilator grid from outside, so it looks as if somebody's come in through there and opened the door. I don't want Dad to think it's me. I'll find it hard enough anyway to look him in the face after this."

"I know how it is, Barry. All right. Now, how shall we signal to you that we've arrived?"

"I don't see how you can," I said. "Let's fix a definite time. I'll open up for you at eleven thirty, provided Dad and Geoff are asleep. If the front door isn't open then, it'll be because the way isn't clear. In that case you'd better wait. Stay around till twelve, after which it'll be too late anyway; there won't be time to finish the job. But I don't think that problem will arise. Everyone'll be tired after the previous night's watch. They'll sleep like babes."

"I hope *you* don't," said Stuart. "It would be funny, or rather, it wouldn't be very funny, if you couldn't let us in because you'd really gone to sleep on watch."

"Don't worry," I said. "I won't be in any state to go to sleep."

"All right, then. See you tomorrow night at eleven thirty. So long, Barry."

" 'Bye, Stuart."

I remembered that there might indeed be people creeping up on us at any time. I took the football rattle in my hand and made a tour of the house, peering out of each window in turn through the cracks between boards or sandbags.

The snow was all gone now, the sky was clear, the moon almost full. The firs and rhododendrons were sharp in outline, though black and impenetrable in substance. At the back, some distance away, could be seen a single lighted window of another house. It seemed only to emphasize the isolation that had first attracted Father to Rose Grove. It was all too easy to imagine people lurking in the shadows. I'd have liked to go outside and walk round the house. That wasn't a sensible thing to do, since I could easily have been jumped by an intruder, and there would then be no watchdog at all; but I was already oppressed by a feeling that we were as much barricaded in as others were barricaded out. Tonight the house felt like a prison of our own devising.

15

FATHER'S ALARM CLOCK RANG at five minutes before one o'clock, and jerked me upright in my chair. I realized that although I hadn't actually been asleep I must have been dozing. I made a final hasty circuit of the house and couldn't see any sign of activity. Father came down at one o'clock exactly, wearing his battle dress top over his pajamas. Round his waist was the belt that carried the holster.

"All quiet?" he asked.

"All quiet," I said.

"Good lad, Barry," said Father, though I hadn't done anything. "Off you go to bed now. If anything happens you'll hear that rattle. But don't think about it, just lie down and get your sleep."

I'd hardly slept the night before, and I was too tired even to undress. I took my outer clothes off, got into bed, and was asleep at once. There was no perceptible gap before Geoff was shaking me and telling me it was after eight o'clock and breakfast was ready. He and Father had left me to sleep while they made it.

"I've just been listening to the radio news," Father said

as I went into the kitchen. "They're still going on about this supposed rescue operation."

"Oh, yes?" I said. "Cliff told me something about that. Is anything settled yet?"

"No," said Father. "They're still arguing. And I don't trust these foreigners from new-rich countries you never heard of until five minutes ago. Maybe they'll sort something out in the end, there's no telling."

Geoff slapped bacon onto our plates.

"All that talk," he said. "Don't count on it."

"Yes, that's the safest principle," said Father. "We still have to look after ourselves. Don't rely on anyone, that's my motto."

After breakfast we checked round our defenses and made some minor improvements and adjustments. Then, like soldiers passing time away in the trenches, we played cards together. Father didn't believe in playing for money, but just to add interest to the game we used some old hundred-pound notes. By midafternoon a certain amount of reaction had set in. The sense of confinement was bothering me a good deal and Geoff a little.

"It's a fine day," Father said. "Why don't you two go out? So long as you're back by dark."

Geoff and I kicked a ball about a bit on the gravel—an activity that was more to his taste than mine. Then there was a Saturday afternoon match he wanted to watch on television. He went in. I wandered round the Mount for an hour. I had an impulse to walk down to Wendy's house, but resisted it. There were feelings of queasy apprehension in my stomach. Ordinary life seemed suspended until the crisis at Rose Grove was over.

By the time the daylight failed, it seemed there must be a power cut in progress. Looking down from the Mount, I couldn't see the usual city lights. From the windows of houses around came the feeble glimmers of oil lamps or candles. It was time I returned to my post. But my feet didn't want to take me, and when I got back to Rose Grove I didn't want to go in. The sense of a self-imposed prison was strong again. I walked round the outside of the house. At the back I became aware of a rustle in the bushes. I moved toward it, and the rustle resolved itself rapidly into a small boy who raced away and disappeared through a hole in the hedge before I could even make up my mind to pursue him.

I knew who it was, of course. It was Mel Holloway again. I was sure the Holloways would be up to something sooner or later. I pondered the possibilities as I made my way to the front door and was admitted by Geoff. And I decided not to mention Mel to Father. There was no point in putting him on the alert. In a few hours' time Share Alike would be here and the problems would all be solved, for better or worse.

Twenty-five past eleven. Geoff had long been in bed. The power cut was over. Father had unexpectedly stayed up a little; I had thought he would want to get as much sleep as possible before his one o'clock watch, but he didn't seem tired and was reminiscing again. This time it wasn't about the war but about the early years of his married life; about Nessie and Geoff and me as small children. I had never thought Father was very interested in children; he had four of them, but looked on them either as part of the furniture or as a source of irritation, according to their degree of activity at any given moment. But he remembered a good deal with pride about Nessie as an exceptionally bright and pretty child and Geoff as an active and energetic one. I had been just ordinary, it appeared.

When eleven o'clock passed, I began to worry. Perhaps Father wouldn't go to bed before his watch at all. But at five past eleven it occurred to me to do the obvious thing, and I asked him if he hadn't better get some sleep. Father looked at the time, was surprised to find how late it was, and said he'd turn in now if I didn't mind. I didn't mind. By twenty past eleven he was audibly asleep.

I got the mallet from the under-stair cupboard, to knock out the props from the front door. It was a more awkward job than I'd expected. Two or three good swipes with the mallet would have done the trick, but would have made too much noise. I tapped lightly, but the props wouldn't move. I tapped a little more strongly, and the sound, though not great, seemed to me to echo through the house. My heart thumped. For a moment I thought I heard somebody stirring in a room above. Then the silence re-formed itself. I remembered what we'd done when putting the props in, and shoved hard against the door, easing the pressure enough for me to get them out with a few more light taps. Silence again, and the door was unblocked. It was fully half past eleven.

I peered out into the night. It was brighter, if anything, than the night before. The moon was full and was unclouded. Outbuildings cast sharp, angled shadows on the gravel. Once again the rhododendrons, though clear in outline, seemed to soak away the moonlight, and there were caverns of blackness beneath them. Nobody could be seen. I felt again the urge to walk around outside, but I resisted it and went back to my chair in the front sitting room. A minute later I heard the sound of a vehicle being driven slowly and gently into our drive. I looked out through one of the cracks. It was a closed van, without lights and without any name on its side. It nosed its way to the side of the house and out of my line of sight.

That must be Share Alike. I nearly went round to open the door. But I was prevented by an illogical feeling that actually letting in the invaders myself would be the final act of treachery. Stuart knew the front door would be open. They could make their own way in. I felt slightly sickened already by my part in the episode. Whatever the arguments, the fact remained that Father had trusted me and I had let him down.

Two or three minutes passed. No further sound. Perhaps they were sitting in or standing around the van, planning how they'd carry out the operation. It seemed odd that they didn't come in, though. Another minute or two of silence. I got up and headed for the front door after all, wondering why the delay. And at that moment I heard sounds at last: first a series of crunching noises from the back of the house; then from below me, at basement level, a clatter as of something metallic hitting a hard floor. They were breaking into the cellar itself. Probably pushing in the ventilator, as I'd told Stuart they should do. But why on earth did they have to do that first? Surely Stuart had understood what I meant. The front door was the simple and obvious way in. They could have dealt with the ventilator grid later.

Anyway, I must go down to them. I descended the cellar steps. There was darkness down there, broken by the moving flashes from an electric torch.

"Hang on!" I called softly. "I'll put the light on for you."

My fingers groped for the switch. The light came on. A dim light, but enough to show clearly the man who was advancing toward me carrying the flashlight.

"Hello, hello!" he said. "Young Barry, if my eyes don't deceive me. How are you, Barry?" It was Vince Holloway.

I hadn't even brought the football rattle down to the cellar. I turned tail instantly, leaped up the steps three at a time, headed for the front sitting room, and picked up the rattle. I had just time to swing it round my head, making a brief but shattering din, before Vince jumped in and grabbed it from me.

"Silly things, those," he said cheerfully. "I won't let young Mel have one." Then he was holding my arms, and when I tried to kick him he caught hold of a foot and tipped me on my back. And a few seconds later I was on the ground, powerless, and Vince was sitting on me comfortably. "When I'm not so busy," he said, "I'll show you how to do that. It isn't difficult. Might come in handy sometime."

Out in the hall, there was now a confusion of footsteps, some clattering up from below, some coming down from above. Voices were raised, among them Father's, demanding to know what was going on, and broken off in a sharp exclamation of pain. Everything happened quickly, leaving me with a series of disjointed impressions. Scuffling sounds from the hallway. Geoff thrust in through the sitting room door, propelled from behind by somebody who'd pinned his arms behind his back. More scuffling sounds, and a thud that sounded like somebody hitting the floor hard. A swearword or two, and a shouted warning to somebody to watch out. Father yelling, "Barry!" Figures struggling in the doorway. A clatter, and Father's revolver on the floor. Somebody kicking it into a corner. Father held between two men, still trying to lash out, his battle dress torn, his nose bloody. Then order restored and a new picture forming itself, with Vince and his associates in control.

"Hey, look at this!" said one of the men holding Father. "He drew a gun on us!"

"You got it from him pretty smartly, didn't you?" Vince said. "Here, let's have a look." Somebody picked up the revolver and passed it to him. Vince broke it open.

"It's loaded!" he said. For the first time, he looked a little shaken. His friends seemed startled, too, as if a loaded gun was something more dramatic than they'd expected. But Vince recovered quickly.

"You're a determined character, Norman!" he said in an admiring tone.

Father swore at him, in terms I'd never heard from Father before. Vince looked at Father reprovingly.

"Language, language!" he said; and then, "I approve of determination. I don't know that I approve of guns. Dangerous toys, those."

He took the cartridges from the revolver and slipped them into his pocket. Then he tossed the empty gun two or three times from one hand to the other. "Makes me feel like I was in the movies," he said. He went on, very relaxed, "You should have done as I told you, Norman. You should have done a nice peaceful deal in Swiss francs, and saved trouble all round. You've lost out now. You can't appeal to law and order, because you're on the wrong side of it."

"Oh, come on, Vince!" said one of the other men. There were four of them, two now holding Father and one each Geoff and myself. "Let's get moving. What are we going to do with these three?"

"There's no hurry, we've got all night," Vince said. He was obviously enjoying himself, as he'd done when he put his proposition to Father a few nights earlier. "You understand, Norman, that basically we're businessmen. We're not a *gang*." He pronounced the last word with humorous distaste. "Look, you can help yourself and us by being cooperative. Why don't you and the boys just sit quietly and let us get on with the job?"

Father swore at him again.

"Still better," Vince went on unperturbed, "why don't you give us a hand with loading the stuff? And in exchange we'll leave you a bit of it. You'll still be better off than most people. I reckon that's a fair offer, Norman. If I was you, I'd snap it up."

With a sudden burst of energy, Father broke free from the two men who were holding him. There was another scuffle before he was overpowered.

"I've had enough of this, Vince!" said one of the two. He mopped his cheek, which had been cut or scratched. "Let's deal with them."

"All right," Vince said. "Norman, we're going to tie you up. If you struggle any more, we'll hit you over the head first. So do me a favor and take it easy now." He put

232

the gun on a shelf, behind an ornament, and felt in his pocket for some cord.

Vince had said there was all night. But I knew, as nobody else in the room did, that if plans were carried out there wasn't all night at all. I wished desperately that Share Alike would arrive, and in sufficient strength. It must be a quarter to twelve by now. Perhaps they wouldn't come; perhaps they weren't organized enough. I'd listened anxiously for them while Vince was talking. And as the further brief scuffle with Father was going on, I thought I heard in the background the arrival of another vehicle. But no one else seemed to notice it. Maybe I was mistaken.

Then, as Vince moved round behind Father with the cord to tie his hands, I knew I'd been right. There were barely perceptible sounds from the front hall, furtive sounds. Somebody groping around and putting a foot wrong, somebody whispering. There were people in the hall, trying not to wake anyone up.

Vince and his friends were as much taken by surprise as I had been twenty minutes earlier. They stared at each other.

"Come here!" I yelled at the top of my voice.

The man who was holding me put a hand over my mouth, but it was too late. A voice from the hall called, "Barry?" And in came Stuart and half a dozen young men from Share Alike. Whether they knew Vince Holloway or not, it was obvious at a glance that Father and Geoff and I were held captive. Another struggle followed. It was even more one-sided than the previous one, because the Vince group were outnumbered and not at all eager for more fighting. They'd come prepared to deal forcibly if necessary with us three, but not to do battle against odds. After two or three minutes the position had been reversed. One of the men broke out of the room, and I could hear him being pursued through the house. Vince and the other three stood quietly, not resisting. Vince was still calm and self-possessed. I admired his nerve.

"All right," he said to the two young men of student age who were holding his wrists. "You can let go now. Nothing's going to happen." His tone of voice was one of authority, and they did as they were told.

"Who the hell are you?" Stuart Hazell asked Vince.

"They broke in," I said. "They were trying to rob us."

"I'm a businessman," said Vince coolly. "In present conditions, business sometimes has to be done in unorthodox ways. It's as simple as that. Now, who the hell are *you?*"

"We're Share Alike," Stuart said.

"Share Alike! The people who were handing out potatoes in the marketplace the other week?"

"Yes."

"You're not planning to hand this lot out in the marketplace?"

"We haven't decided yet how we'll distribute it."

"Who says you'll distribute anything?" demanded Father. But for the moment nobody was taking notice of him.

"You're giving it away *free?*" said Vince. He sounded shocked. "That's criminal. There's a fortune here. You can't just give it away."

"That's what we're for," said Stuart coldly.

"Why don't we do a deal?" said Vince. "I can dispose of the stuff. And very advantageously."

"Certainly not," said Stuart, more coldly still.

"Don't *I* have anything to do with it?" asked Father.

"Seems not, Norman," said Vince. "No Swiss francs for anyone." As usual, he recovered equanimity quickly. "Oh, well, a good maxim in business is 'Cut your losses.' You can't win every time. This time we've lost. We'd better go."

"Do we let them go?" asked one of the Share Alikers.

"You might as well, mightn't you?" said Vince. "What can you do with us if you don't?"

The Share Alike members looked at one another uncertainly. Nobody was clearly in command. Eventually Stuart said, "Oh, let them go. He's quite right, there's nothing we can do with them. We can't call the police."

The young men watching Vince and his friends seemed glad to have orders of some kind. One of them motioned the four away. It was Tony, who'd been one of the guards on my first meals-on-wheels tour.

Stuart was now taking charge.

"I suppose that's your van round the side?" he said to Vince.

Vince nodded.

"All right. Out through the front door. Take it and go. Tony, will you watch them and see that they do?"

Vince walked out with perfect self-possession. His associates, one of whom had a cut cheek and another a still-bleeding nose, followed him, looking much less cool.

"Listen to me, Stuart Whatsit!" Father said. His tone of voice was indignant. He didn't seem grateful for having been delivered from Vince. "You've no more right to be here than they have. I'll thank you to leave my premises at once!"

"I'm sorry, Mr. Mortimer," Stuart said, "but we've come here to do a job."

"Do a job! Yes, that's the right way to put it. A burglary!"

"You know quite well what the aims of Share Alike are. We've decided we had to act. Are you going to help or hinder us?"

"I'm certainly not going to help you," said Father. "And I'd like to know how you got in."

Stuart was giving nothing away.

"We found a way in," he said. "It doesn't matter how. But, Mr. Mortimer, I'd like to ask you just once more to accept our good faith and let us act with your consent rather than against your will."

"Never!" said Father. "This is my house. These are my boys. Down there are my stocks, built up by me when other folk were taking no thought for the morrow. They're mine." His voice was rising wildly. "Everything here is mine!"

"Sorry, Mr. Mortimer," Stuart said. "I haven't time to discuss the matter anymore. We'll have to start work now."

"Oh, will you?" Father leaped forward. But Tony and Mike, whom I'd met at the center from time to time, had been watching him closely, and now they seized his arms and held him back.

"We'd better take him down to the basement with us," Stuart said. "Don't hurt him, just restrain him."

Mike and Tony led Father away. I saw his eyes travel to

the shelf where the revolver lay unnoticed behind a vase, but he didn't try to get near it. Geoff and I were taken down to the basement, too. Stuart gave no sign that he and I were in collusion.

The next stage of the operation had clearly been worked out in advance. Perhaps the same method had been used in other places. The Share Alikers—some fifteen or eighteen young men and women—formed a chain, leading up the cellar steps, through the passageway and hall, and out to their van which stood in front of the house. And before Father's eyes they began passing his stores up from the cellar and away.

Out went case after case of cans, the ham and corned beef and meatballs and pilchards and condensed milk. Out went the plastic sacks of rice and the dried potatoes. Out went the cocoa and chocolate and coffee, the jars of meat extract and peanut butter, the dried fruit. Out went the drums of cooking oil.

Father's eyes followed each successive item as it moved along the chain and away out of sight. Areas of shelving began to clear, like sands when the tide has gone. I wondered if he would make further attempts to break free, but he must have realized that it wouldn't be any use. He stood in quiet agony, almost dignity, with Mike and Tony at each side of him. At one point Stuart asked if he would rather be in a different room, but Father said in a barely audible voice that he would stay where he was. Tony and Mike came to the alert when he put out a hand to each side, but relaxed when they saw that he was merely taking hold of my hand and Geoff's.

"Well," he said, "we did our best."

"The bastards!" said Geoff fiercely.

"Cool it, kid," said Tony.

Then there was a shout from somewhere above. The movement of stores along the chain halted, went into reverse. Stuart leaped up the cellar steps three at a time. There were shouts, trampling, confusion for the third time in the night. Stuart yelled down the steps, "Everybody up! Raiders!"

The young people who'd formed the cellar end of the chain broke line and hurried away up the steps. Tony, Bill, and the other two who'd been guarding us seemed uncertain for a moment, then must have decided we could hardly do any harm, and followed the rest. Geoff ran upstairs behind them. Father seemed dazed. I took his arm and we followed more slowly.

The hall and passageway were clear now, but the backs of three or four people could be seen in the open front doorway. Beyond were sounds of shouting and of boots crunching on gravel. I led Father into the empty front sitting room where we'd been a few minutes before. He walked with painful slowness to his favorite chair and sat in it, but in an upright posture, not relaxed.

"Are you all right?" I asked him.

"I am perfectly well," he said in a flat, detached voice, as if he didn't really know or care what he was saying. I thought he was suffering from shock. But I didn't want to linger with him; I wanted to know what was going on outside.

"You're worn out," I said. "Try to take it easy."

I left the room and ran to the front door. In clear light the scene was almost as plain as by day. The open back of the Share Alike van, with its floor at waist height, was a few feet away from the door. Three or four young men were inside it, trying to ward off a little crowd of attackers. The main body of raiders, maybe twenty-five or thirty of them, were farther away, in a rough cluster in the middle of the front lawn, with a few of them moving raggedly round toward the side of the house.

It wasn't exactly a battle, because most of the raiders obviously hadn't come in search of a fight. They were leaving that to those who liked it. What they wanted, presumably, was loot. Most were armed with sticks or bottles, though some were carrying their bottles carefully and taking swigs at them from time to time. A few had found stones in the garden and were throwing them in the general direction of our front door. Jim Alsop appeared in front of the mob, shouting to them to stop throwing. They were as likely to hit their own people as the Share Alike defenders.

As I watched, the Share Alike driver ran round the side of the van, opened the cab door, and tried to climb in. Half a dozen raiders ran up and pulled him back. He struggled with them, and clearly wasn't going to make it. Something flew through the air toward the house door, catching a glint of moonlight as it went. It was a ring with the car keys on it. Geoff, standing beside me, dived and picked it up before the three or four people in the doorway had realized what was happening. Briefly the driver was the focus of a scrum; then it broke up, leaving him on the ground. He picked himself up a few seconds later, apparently not much hurt.

The struggle in the open back of the Share Alike van resolved itself into a defense of the stores inside it by a handful of Share Alikers against two or three times as many raiders. Before long the defenders were dragged down into the throng, and raiders clambered on board and began seizing the contents of the van. It seemed to be a case of each for himself, with some of the raiders dragging sacks or drums away to their private caches in dark corners of the garden. The defenders were released, because those who'd grabbed them were more interested in looting the van than in holding them, but they weren't armed in any way and they couldn't push their way back to the van. Some of the attackers engaged in tussles among themselves, like battling housewives in a bargain basement at a sale.

The driver reappeared among the group of Share Alikers in the doorway of the house.

"Anybody got my keys?" he asked.

Geoff handed them to him.

"Half a minute, Dave," said Stuart. "This time, let me come with you."

The two of them crept warily round the blind side of the van, and then across the front of it. Dave made a dash for the cab, and was seen by two or three raiders, but Stuart held them off until he could get inside and lock the door. In a second or two I heard the engine start. The van began to move. Jim Alsop and a few others stood in front of it, blocking its way. Very slowly, Dave edged it forward. Stores were still being thrown out of the back. The van was pushing against people, not giving way but not going fast enough to run them down. Then Dave was clear, and accelerated. A few last raiders threw bags, bins, and cases out of the back and jumped after them. The van moved off down the drive. I couldn't see how much of the contents was still inside it, but my guess was that most had gone. Share Alike wouldn't get much of a haul from that van.

As the van drove away, Stuart and Jim Alsop faced each other. Stuart shouted something. Jim shouted something back, then moved in on Stuart. It looked as though there'd be a hand-to-hand fight between them.

Then a shot rang out. Both started back. There was another shot, then another, and Stuart fell.

For a few seconds, that stopped everything. Nobody knew where the shot had come from. Two of the Share Alikers ran forward unhindered and bent down over Stuart. Geoff and I looked at each other and without saying anything hurried into the house. We pushed our way through the press of people in the hall, and went into the sitting room. Father was holding out the revolver at arm's length, the barrel pointing out an opened window through a gap between two sandbags. The room smelled like Guy Fawkes Night.

"Oh, my God!" I exclaimed. I ought to have remembered the gun, and to have known that Father would have more ammunition for it.

"Dad! Stop!" Geoff shouted.

Father lowered the gun for a moment.

"The other's the one I really want," he said. "That Alsop fellow."

"What do you mean?" demanded Geoff. "You're mad!"

Father looked in fact curiously calm, and his voice had a lifeless, matter-of-fact tone.

"Not that the do-gooder's much better," he said. "He deserved what he got. But the moment I get a clear line on that Alsop . . ."

He raised the revolver again. His finger was on the trigger.

Geoff dashed forward and grabbed the gun. The barrel rose at an angle, the gun fired, and a bullet went into the ceiling. Geoff broke the gun open, unloaded it, and threw it down on the floor. Then he took Father by the shoulders and shook him. Geoff had been bigger than Father for some time, but Father was so dominant in the family that until this moment the fact had never sunk in.

"You're out of your wits!" Geoff shouted. "What if you've killed Stuart? What if you'd killed them both? You're a menace. You're a bloody madman!"

"Between them they've cost me everything," Father said in the same flat tone. "A bullet each is what they deserve. And Gerald Bowling another. And Vince Holloway another."

Geoff shook him again, furiously.

"I've finished with you!" he said. "You're no father of mine. And I'm the last. I know what Barry thinks. You've lost us, Dad. You've lost us all. Who are you protecting now?"

Geoff turned to me. He seemed to have gained authority in the last few minutes.

"Now!" he said. "What's happened to Stuart?"

Stuart wasn't dead, or, it seemed, badly injured. He had walked into the house, white and shaky, leaning on Mike's arm. On the opposite shoulder his shirt was stained with blood, but it looked as if he had only a flesh wound.

"Where's Ron Kellar?" somebody was shouting, and voices picked up the call, "Ron Kellar! Ron Kellar!"

"Take Stuart to the kitchen! Give him a cup of tea!" Geoff said; and then he himself joined in the shout, "Ron Kellar! Where's Ron Kellar?"

Ron Kellar came hurrying to the kitchen. I knew him slightly. He was a junior doctor at the Royal Infirmary.

"All right, Stuart," he said. "Something tells me you haven't finished with life's troubles yet. You'll live to get into plenty more. Now let's have a look at it."

I picked my way through to the front door again. The silence that followed the gunshots had lasted until Stuart reached the house. Then the noise broke out again, but the skirmishing was temporarily at a halt. The defenders had all fallen back into the doorway, and it wasn't clear at first whether the raiders would try to force a way in. Some had made off already with their gains. Others were still swigging from bottles. My guess was that they'd raided a package store before coming here. Obviously none of them could be sure that there was anything still in the house worth fighting for.

Then someone came round from the back and started telling Jim Alsop something. What it was, I couldn't hear above the general noise. But I could guess. One of the raiders who'd straggled round the side of the house had found the missing ventilator grid, made a way in, and seen that a large quantity of stores still remained inside.

Jim Alsop shouted to the raiders. Probably he was telling them to put down their bottles or their booty, for a few of them did so. Then there was a surge toward the front door. The few Share Alikers still outside it, and I, hurried inside. We slammed the door behind us. Somebody turned the key in the lock and shot the bolt. Almost at once there were two or three heavy thuds on the door from the other side. It shuddered but didn't give.

The Share Alikers were hardly more organized than the mob, especially since Stuart had been put out of action. A few of them made ineffectual attempts to block the door. Somebody was trying to drag up a heavy piece of furniture, and merely getting in everyone's way. Nobody had grasped the purpose of the posts that were fixed across the door and hallway, and it wouldn't have been any good if they had, because the key pieces of timber which I'd tapped out of place and left lying in the hall had been taken by somebody for use as weapons. There was no telling where they were now.

As the thudding on the door began again, two or three defenders leaned with their backs against it. That didn't seem a very effective method. It was doubtful whether the door could resist a determined attack. And another thought was on my mind.

"The ventilator!" I shouted. "The basement ventilator!"

Nobody knew what I meant. Geoff joined me, shouting and then trying to explain at the tops of our voices. It seemed to take a long time to convey the idea that raiders could be coming in one at a time through the gap where the ventilator grid had been. And when at last we got our message across, it was altogether too effective. The thudding on the front door had ceased for the moment. And all but one or two of the people inside moved, in an unthinking surge, back through the hall and passageway and down into the cellar. A few raiders had indeed got in through the ventilator gap, but they weren't finding it easy to remove the spoils, because you couldn't clamber up to the gap with any sizable amount of stuff in your arms, and those inside didn't trust those waiting above. Skirmishing broke out in the cellar, with the Share Alikers at an advantage and the raiders inclined to look for escape rather than to stay and fight.

Then there was a great crash from above, and a clatter of boots along the passageway. I knew what had happened. A combined assault, perhaps with something used as a battering ram, had broken open the front door. And now the raiders came through in force, pouring down the cellar steps. They didn't bother to attack anybody, they just made straight for the racks. A few Share Alike people tried to fend them off, but there were too many. They were swarming everywhere. Stacks crashed down, there was fighting over desirable spoils, nobody could tell who was on whose side. People trying to make their way out with sacks or cases got into tangles with others still trying to get at the spoils. Two or three raiders had made arrangements with friends outside, and passed things up through the gap after all.

Cans rolled around underfoot and brought unwary raiders down amid the curses of others. Discovery of Father's remaining stock of spirits brought a thick, fighting cluster of looters to one corner of the cellar. Raiders opened bottles on the spot, often by knocking necks against the wall. Drink poured down throats or on the floor. The reek began to spread through the cellars. Somebody pushed a rack over, to get at something underneath, and scores of glass jars crashed to the concrete floor.

Compared with the neat operation of Share Alike, it was an appallingly inefficient way of emptying a cellar. But gradually everything went. There was nobody to call the Share Alikers off, but nobody to urge them on, either. With so much broken glass around, so many heavy cans, so many people wielding bottles and more than half drunk, it was all too easy to get hurt, by accident rather than by anybody's intent. In twos and threes, the

Share Alike people gradually ebbed away, and they could hardly be blamed, for there was little they could do if they stayed. You could tell them apart from the raiders as they went up the cellar steps, because on the whole they were younger, and they were all empty-handed.

As the stores diminished, the throng diminished too. Most of the raiders presumably had got all they wanted or could carry. A noisy few went on drinking and squabbling in the corner where the liquor had been. Father, coming down the steps in a dazed state, was in time to watch the last stages of the sacking of his stronghold, and to see Jim Alsop—ignoring us completely —round up and chivvy away the lingerers.

At length—our eardrums ringing, our noses full of the reek of liquor, our brains battered and dazed—we were left in silence among the ruins. There was litter everywhere. Overturned and splintered racks seemed afloat on a sea of broken glass. Here and there were cans that had been kicked or trampled into crazy shapes. And there were a few undamaged cans left in dark corners, unnoticed. Father, moving with automatic care through the debris, collected a few of these together and placed them, half consciously, in a single, small, pathetic stack in front of him. Then he swung a boot and demolished the pile, like a child grown tired of its building bricks.

"They haven't done themselves any good, you know, taking all this," he said. "They'll be hungry again tomorrow."

16

THE FIRST DAY OF SPRING; and weather, for once, to match. A day of mild and just-perceptible breeze; the year unfreezing, easing, stretching its limbs. After such a winter, one somehow hadn't expected it. But the big neglected gardens on the Mount were splashy with daffodils, and the birds had noticed nothing amiss. Even the Novembral gloom of Rose Grove, enclosed by its dark drooping evergreens, was shot through with the sights and sounds of reviving life.

Geoff and I had gone round the house that morning, unboarding the basement windows, letting the fresh air in. Days before, soon after the attack, we'd opened up the ground floor, removed and emptied out all the sandbags, brushed the broken glass off the cellar floors, restored the racks, washed the whole place down. But the smell of spirits lingered. Today's breeze would clear it away. "A good cellar, this," Geoff had remarked dryly. "Should be useful for something someday."

The small remnants of Father's stores had gone into Mother's pantry to give her a start with her resumed housekeeping. She had of course come back the moment she heard that the house had been raided and that Father

247

was in a state of collapse. "I know now that he can't manage without me," she'd said. "And he knows it, too." Ellen was still at the Timpsons', but was due home today.

In the country at large, things seemed a little more hopeful. The international rescue operation that was supposed to save us was still hanging fire, but talks continued, and it looked as if the politicians of the various countries had agreed on the main issue. If we could once get back on our feet, they believed we could still support ourselves, and that would be better for everybody else as well as us. In the meantime, we needed food and raw materials to be going on with, until we could get our production and exports rolling. The details were still being argued about, but relief ships were said to be laden and waiting at continental ports for the signal to move.

The government obviously expected a positive result, because it had brought out some last-line stocks, and food was a little easier to find. A New Pound was talked of, equivalent to a hundred million old ones. There was even talk of the return of the penny, and it was a long time since you'd been able to buy anything with pennies. Food rations, though small, were once again being honored.

Now I was on my way down to the welfare center to help Cliff. Cliff hadn't been involved in the events at our house, but he'd been hit by them, with Stuart out of action at the center and Father out of action at the shop. Stuart's wound wasn't serious and was mending satisfactorily. He hadn't reported it to anyone and didn't seem to bear any malice. But on Cliff's suggestion Geoff had dropped the revolver in the lake at Ringwood Park, and Father hadn't said anything about that.

I walked down the Mount to meet Cliff at Wendy's house, where he lodged. Wendy was in the tiny front garden when I arrived, at work with a trowel in a flower bed.

"Hello, Wendy."

"Hello, Barry."

"What are you planting?"

"Chrysanthemums."

"Flowers! I'd have thought in these times it would be vegetables. Aren't flowers a bit of a luxury?"

"Yes. But today I just had a feeling as if they were a necessity."

"Hmmm."

"You don't feel that, Barry?"

"Well, I know what you mean by it."

"That's something, then. And I wanted to be outside after the housework. Mother's still getting better, but she's not fit to do anything yet."

"Another time, I'd help you. But just now I have to go down to the center with Cliff."

Wendy was looking at somebody behind me. I turned, and Cliff was there, smiling.

"Too bad about the center," he said. "Actually, I could manage without you at a pinch."

"I wasn't hinting at that, Cliff. I didn't know you were there. Of course I'm coming to the center."

"As a matter of fact," Cliff said, "I'm not ready yet. Why don't you go on ahead of me? And Wendy, you remember I said I'd found a coat for your mum, to replace the one you sold when things were really bad? Well, why don't you go down with Barry and collect it from the center?"

"Sometimes, Cliff," I said, "you're a bit obvious."

"Obvious, nothing," said Cliff. "The doctor told Mrs. Farrar she could go out, but she can't go out at this time of year without a coat, can she? So off you go, young Wendy, and collect it. You don't really *mind* going down to the center with Barry, do you?"

"I can stand it," said Wendy.

We walked through Ringwood, the city's biggest park. It was looking uncared-for. A spreading skin of green covered part of the park lake; unpainted boats were stacked up behind the unpainted boathouse. The grass was long and ragged, uncut for many months; the bedding plants from last summer had never been moved. The city couldn't pay any staff because its taxes were worthless by the time they were collected. But people wanted jobs; they'd be back at work as soon as the crisis ended. In the meantime one realized that Nature could do quite a lot without municipal aid. Like everywhere else that hadn't been covered with concrete, the park was alive with new season's green.

"I'll race you to the other gate," Wendy said, and set off at a run across the grass. But before we'd gone far I realized that she hadn't the strength to keep on running. I stretched out a hand to her as if I were tired myself, and we continued at walking pace.

"You've got your feet wet," I said when we reached the path at the far side.

"So have you."

"Do you mind?"

"No. Do you?"

"No."

She was wearing an old pair of sandals. She took them off and carried them in the hand that wasn't holding mine.

"It's nice to feel the sun on your bare feet," she said.

The queue at the center was as long as ever. But with the arrival of spring it was a little more animated; the old people were no longer huddled in the tight isolation of mufflers and turned-up collars. These were the ones who had survived the winter in a reasonable state of health, and they were congratulating themselves and one another. Mike, who was well known to all of them because he had the unenviable job of cutting off the queue when it grew too long for the number of meals available, was chatting them up this morning.

"We got meat for you today," he said. "Honest we have. Fresh mince. One of these years, if you keep on coming long enough, you'll get steak."

There was unbelieving laughter.

"That'll be the day," said one of the customers.

"But we won't live to see it," said another.

Mike went to find the coat for Wendy's mother. Wendy left with it over her arm, and I worked my stint in the kitchen. On a fine spring day it wasn't the ideal place to be. But I felt extraordinarily happy. Later Cliff drove me round to the shop. The shelves were empty as usual, and Cliff's main duty was to keep the shop open and take a few repair orders while the one remaining girl assistant was out at lunch.

Soon after lunch the area manager arrived, and disappeared with Cliff into the little back office. When they came out, they were both smiling. After the area manager had left, I said, "You look cheerful, Cliff." But he didn't tell me why.

"We'll leave Sheila in charge," he said, "and I'll come up to the Timpsons' with you to collect Ellen and take her home."

Ellen wept, and flung her arms round Mrs. Timpson's neck. She'd been happy there. She wanted to be with her mother, but she didn't want to leave the Timpsons, or Nessie. Couldn't Mother go back there, she asked, instead of her having to go to Rose Grove? The rest of us could visit them when we wanted. According to Ellen, Peggy liked being with the Timpsons, too. Ellen didn't say so, but it was clear that she felt uneasy about being under the same roof as Father again, even though he'd agreed to have Peggy back and had shown no surprise on learning where she was.

In the end Nessie volunteered to come with Ellen and see her comfortably settled. She also said she'd get a promise from Father that she could visit Ellen as often as they both wanted. That reassured Ellen. In the car she insisted that Nessie should sit beside her. I sat at the front with Cliff.

Father came to the door to greet us. Since the siege he had been withdrawn, silent, sunk in apathy. Today he was a little brighter, a little more like his old self. He seemed pleased to see Ellen, who submitted reluctantly to his embrace. We all went into the sitting room, where he sat in his favorite chair. Ellen, on the sofa, sat between Mother and Nessie, and drew an arm of each around her. I'd put out her old teddy bear, which she'd left behind when she went to the Timpsons', but she didn't notice it.

Father seemed pleased to see Nessie, too. He asked after Terry, and repeated his suggestion that Terry should come in under his umbrella; it seemed momentarily to escape his notice that he no longer had an umbrella to offer. Nessie said she didn't think Terry would leave his mother at present. Then Father asked if Nessie herself would come back, and she said she didn't think so. Father considered this for a moment.

"I suppose you'll be getting married," he said then.

"I don't know," Nessie said. "Maybe. We haven't really thought about it."

"Oh, well," said Father after a further pause, "we have to get used to new ways. I must say, I find it hard. Nothing's what it used to be. Take the firm. It's not the same since Mr. Edward and Mr. Gerald left."

"Mr. Gerald's a crook," said Geoff.

"No, no," said Father. "I thought that myself for a time, I admit. But there must have been some mistake. I must have misunderstood what he was saying. He couldn't *really* have meant to blackmail me. Not Mr. Gerald. Mr. Gerald's a gentleman, a real gentleman. I hope I haven't frightened him away for good. They don't make them like that anymore."

"Thank God," said Nessie quietly, but Father didn't seem to hear.

"Anyway," he went on, "even if the firm's not what it used to be, I still owe it some loyalty. I believe in loyalty, you know. Now I'm feeling a bit better, I think I'll get back to the shop on Monday. It isn't as if there was a huge amount of work to do. It won't be a great strain. How are things these days, Clifford?"

"Oh, pretty quiet, Mr. Mortimer. But the area manager was in today. The big chiefs think the rescue operation will go ahead, and they're planning for the future already. They'll probably open two or three new stores in this region."

"You know, Clifford," Father said thoughtfully, "you're a good lad. Reliable. If there's any justice, you'll get promotion one of these days."

"Well, as a matter of fact," Cliff said, "the area manager told me I'm in line for it. He says I'll be given charge of one of the new stores."

"That's splendid, Clifford. I shall miss you, of course, but I'm glad for your sake. And Clifford, let me give you a word of advice. As soon as you can afford it, get married. I know there are some of the younger generation who think it doesn't matter—" he looked meaningfully across at Nessie—"but if you ask me, there's nothing like marriage. It steadies a man. I got married, and I've never regretted it."

"I don't think the person I'd like to marry would marry me," Cliff said. Unlike Father, he didn't even glance at Nessie. And Nessie said, impersonally, as if it had nothing to do with her, "I should think a sensible girl would marry you, Cliff. Some girls aren't sensible, that's all."

"Oh, well," Cliff said. "Mustn't complain." And then, "I'm intruding on a family occasion. I ought to be on my way."

When Cliff left, Father's brief spell of animation came to an end. He sank back in his chair and for a while sat silent, looking at nothing in particular. He seemed shrunken: an old defeated man. At last he said, "There was a time when I didn't think I'd see you all around me again. Now here we are. But it's not the same, is it? It'll never be the same again."

He looked into our faces.

"I tried to see you through," he said. "I did my best. I did my best for all of you, didn't I?"

Nessie, Geoff, and I glanced at one another. We didn't know what to say. It was Mother who reassured him.

"Yes, love, yes," she said. "You did your best."

"It sounds from the news bulletins," Father said, "as if all this trouble is going to be sorted out. I always thought it would. I knew it was a matter of holding on, however long it took. And I held on while I could. I did what I thought was right. I didn't let you down, did I?" His voice was anxious.

"No, love, no," said Mother. "You didn't let us down."

"I've often told you how, when I was a boy, my dad let us down. He did, you know. Had a business and drank the profits. We often went hungry, often and often. I made up my mind when I was married, none of my family would go hungry, whatever happened. And you didn't, did you? Nobody's ever gone hungry in my house."

"Not for food," said Nessie quietly.

"What was that? What did you say, Agnes?"

"Nothing," said Nessie. "Nothing."

About the Author

JOHN ROWE TOWNSEND has had a lifelong interest in children's books. He is the author of two books on children's literature, *Written for Children* and *A Sense of Story,* and the editor of an anthology, *Modern Poetry.* His novels, published in England and the United States, include the three books in the "Jungle Trilogy"—*Pirate's Island, Trouble in the Jungle* (originally *Gumble's Yard*), and *Good-bye to the Jungle.* All three were chosen by the American Library Association as notable books of the years in which they appeared. In 1963 his *Hell's Edge* was a runner-up for the Carnegie Medal, and *The Intruder,* a Carnegie honors-list book for 1969, won the 1970 *Boston Globe–Horn Book* Award for excellence of text and an Edgar from the Mystery Writers of America. His two most recent books were *Forest of the Night* and *The Summer People. Saturday Review* has said of *The Summer People*: "A gracefully written novel . . . a well-sustained mood that captures and surrounds its reader." It was chosen by the American Library Association as a notable book published in the year 1972.